HENRIETTA WHO?

HENRIETTA WHO?

Catherine Aird

Chivers Press • G.K. Hall & Co.
Bath, England   Thorndike, Maine USA

This Large Print edition is published by Chivers Press, England, and by G.K. Hall & Co., USA.

Published in 2000 in the U.K. by arrangement with the author, c/o Gillon Aitken.

Published in 2000 in the U.S. by arrangement with Gillon Aitken Associates.

U.K. Hardcover   ISBN 0-7540-4123-9   (Chivers Large Print)
U.K. Softcover   ISBN 0-7540-4124-7   (Camden Large Print)
U.S. Softcover   ISBN 0-7838-9003-6   (Nightingale Series Edition)

The text of this Large Print edition is unabridged.
Other aspects of the book may vary from the original edition.

Set in 16 pt. New Times Roman.

Printed in Great Britain on acid-free paper.

British Library Cataloguing in Publication Data available

Library of Congress Cataloging-in-Publication Data

Aird, Catherine.
     Henrietta who? / Catherine Aird.
       p.   cm.
     ISBN 0-7838-9003-6 (lg. print : sc : alk. paper)
     1. Sloan, C. D. (Fictitious character)—Fiction.
     2. Police—England—Fiction. 3. England—Fiction.
     4. Large type books. I. Title.
     PR6051.I65 H4   2000
     823'.914—dc21   00–021437

For all my eleven o'clock friends, with love

CHAPTER ONE

Harry Ford was a postman. He was a postman of a vintage that is fast disappearing—that is to say he still did his delivery round on a bicycle. The little red vans had reached the large village of Down Martin but his own round of the smaller ones like Larking and Belling St Peter was just as quick on two wheels as on four.

And he, for one, wasn't sorry. Gave you time to think, did a bicycle, even if it was a bit chilly at six o'clock of a dank morning in March. He was well muffled up against the cold though and he didn't mind the half dark. Besides, there were compensations. Another few weeks and he'd be abroad in that glorious early morning light that did something for the soul.

He braked gently as he coasted round the corner into Larking. He knew exactly where to brake on this road. In fact, there wasn't much of the village he didn't know after delivering its mail all these years.

An outsider would have said Larking was typical of a thousand other English villages. And, as it happened, this was true, though the people of Larking wouldn't have liked it. It had all the appurtenances of a normal village and the usual complement of important—and self-important—people: two different groups,

Spiritual leadership was provided by the Reverend Edward Bouverie Meyton. He lived at the Rectory on the green by the church (one Diocesan leaflet, three appeals, a Missionary newsletter, the quarterly report of the Additional Curates' Society and an interesting letter from the Calleshire Historical Association).

Secular leadership came from James Augustus Heber Hibbs, Esquire, at The Hall (an assortment of bills, two closely typed pages of good advice from his stockbroker, a wine list, a picture postcard from his cousin Maude, and a letter from Scotland about a grouse moor).

Harry Ford, postman, was not deceived. He knew as well as anyone else that real power—as opposed to leadership—was vested behind the counter at the Post Office cum General Store in the vast person of Mrs Ricks (one seed catalogue: Mrs Ricks rarely committed herself to paper). A sharp eye and a sharper tongue made her a force to be reckoned with.

Larking shared a branch of the Women's Institute with the neighbouring hamlet of Belling St Peter (Mrs Hibbs was President), and a doctor with a cluster of small communities round about.

And everyone thought they knew everything about everyone else.

In which they were very mistaken.

2

Harry Ford looked at the Post Office clock—dimly visible through the uncurtained window—though only from habit. He had done the round so often that he didn't need a clock to know that, saving Christmas and a General Election, he would finish his Larking delivery at a quarter to eight in the furthest farmhouse, where—letters or not—he would fetch up in the kitchen with a cup of scalding tea.

Only it didn't work out that way this morning.

For ever afterwards he was thankful that he had been on his bicycle and not in a little red van. If he had been in a van, as he frequently reiterated in the days that followed, he couldn't possibly have avoided the huddled figure that was lying in the road.

'Right on the corner at the far end of the village,' he said breathlessly into the telephone after he had taken one quick look and pedalled furiously back to the telephone kiosk outside the post office. 'Lying in the road. Do come quickly,' he implored the man at the ambulance station. 'If anything else comes round the bend they won't be able to avoid her either.'

'Where exactly?' demanded the voice at the other end. Larking was deep in rural Calleshire and the whole of that part of the country was an intricate network of minor roads. And it wasn't really light yet.

'Through Larking village proper,' said Ford, 'and out on the other road to Belling St Peter.'

'The other road?' countered the man on the telephone, who had been caught out by bad directions before.

'Not the main road to Belling. The back road. Come to Larking Post Office and then fork left and she's about a quarter of a mile down the road on the bad bend.'

'Right you are. You get back to her then.' The duty man on the Berebury Ambulance Station switchboard flipped a lever which connected him with the crew room. 'Emergency just come in, Fred. Back of beyond, I'm afraid. Woman lying in the road.'

'Dead?'

'Caller didn't say she was alive,' he said reasonably, 'and he didn't mention injuries. Just that she was lying in the road.'

'Dead then,' said the experienced Fred.

'Or drunk,' said the man in charge who had been at the game even longer.

She wasn't drunk.

Harry Ford going back to have a second, more considered look decided that beyond any doubt at all she was dead. He had been almost sure the first time by the inadequate gleam of his bicycle lamp but now with the sky growing lighter every minute he was absolutely certain.

Her Majesty's Mails being his prime concern he propped his bicycle safely in the deep hedge, that same deep hedge that made

4

this a blind corner, then he came back and stood squarely in the middle of the road. He would be seen by anyone coming now. Not, he decided, that there was ever likely to be much traffic on this road—still less so early in the morning.

This line of thought proved productive.

Not only, now he came to think of it, would there be almost no vehicles using this road first thing in the morning but it was equally unlikely that anyone would be walking along it.

Still less a woman.

A man, perhaps, walking up to one of the farms to do the milking, but not a woman.

He considered in his mind the houses beyond. There were about six of them before you could say you were really out of Larking and then there was a two-mile stretch with just three big farms, then Belling St Peter.

Harry Ford advanced a little.

He might know her himself come to that—he knew most Larking people.

But he hadn't taken more than a step when he heard something coming. It was too soon for the ambulance; besides the direction was wrong. He cocked his head, listening. It wasn't a car either, he decided, getting out into the middle of the road ready to wave anything on wheels to a standstill. Quite suddenly the oncoming noise resolved itself into a tractor which pulled up to a quick halt as the driver saw him.

'Accident?' shouted the man at the wheel above the engine noise.

' 'Fraid so,' shouted back Ford.

The tractor engine spluttered and died and there was a sudden silence.

'She's dead,' said Ford.

The young man got down from his high seat. It was one of the sons of the farmer from further down the road, by the name of Bill Thorpe.

'I found her,' said Ford.

Not that it looked as if she'd been hit by a bicycle.

'She's from one of the cottages, isn't she?' said Thorpe, peering down. 'You know, Harry, I think I know who she is.'

Ford, who to tell the truth hadn't been all that keen on having a really close look on his own, was emboldened by the presence of the young man and bent down towards the cold white face. 'Why, it's Mrs Jenkins.'

'That's right,' said Thorpe.

'Boundary Cottage,' responded the postman automatically. (The odd letter, no circulars, very few bills.)

Thorpe looked round. 'Hit and run,' he said bitterly. 'Not even a ruddy skid mark.'

'It's a nasty corner,' offered Ford.

Thorpe was still looking at the road. 'You can see where he hit the verge a bit afterwards and straightened up again.'

Ford didn't know much about cars. 'Too

fast?'

'Too careless.'

'You'd have thought anyone would have seen her,' agreed Ford.

'Walking on the wrong side, though.'

'Depends whether she was coming or going,' said Ford, who was the slower thinker of the two.

'I should have said she was walking home,' pronounced Thorpe carefully. 'Last night.'

'Last night?' Ford looked shocked.

'If that mark on the grass is his front tyre after he hit her then she was walking along the left-hand side of the road towards her home.'

'But last night,' insisted Ford. 'You mean she's been here all night?'

Thorpe scratched an intelligent forehead. 'I don't know, Harry, but she isn't likely to have been walking home this morning in the dark, is she?'

Harry Ford shook his head. 'A very quiet lady, I'd have said.'

'And,' continued Thorpe, pursuing his theory, 'if she'd been going anywhere very early she'd have been walking the other way. No, I'd say myself she was going home last night.'

'Off the last bus, perhaps,' suggested the postman.

'Perhaps.'

'Her daughter's not at home then,' said Ford firmly. 'Otherwise she'd have been out looking for her.'

'No, she's away still. Back at the end of term.' He looked down at the still figure in the road and said, 'Sooner now.'

'I rang the ambulance,' said Ford, for want of something to say.

Thorpe moved with sudden resolution. 'Well, then, I'll go and ring the police. Don't you let them move her until they come.'

'Right.'

Thorpe paused, one foot on the tractor step. 'Poor Henrietta. No father and now no mother either.'

* * *

Police-Constable Hepple came over from Down Martin on his motor-cycle and measured the road and drew chalk lines round the body and finally allowed the ambulance men to take it away. He, too, knew Mrs Jenkins by sight.

'Widow, isn't she, Harry?' he said to the postman.

'That's right. Just the one girl.'

He got out his notebook. 'Does she know about this?'

'She's away,' volunteered young Thorpe. 'At university.'

'Do you know her exact address?'

But young Thorpe went a bit pink and said rather distantly that he did not. So PC Hepple made another note and then measured the tyre mark on the grass verge.

'I'd say a five-ninety by fourteen myself,' offered Thorpe, who was keen on cars. 'That's a big tyre on a big car.' Now that the body had gone he could talk about that more freely too. 'Those were big car injuries she had.'

PC Hepple, who had reached much the same conclusions himself, nodded.

' 'Tisn't what you'd call a busy road,' went on Thorpe.

'Busy!' snorted Harry Ford. 'I shouldn't think it gets more than a dozen cars a day.'

'Even the milk lorries all go the other way,' said Thorpe, 'because it's a better road.'

'Did you have any visitors at the farm last night?' Hepple asked Thorpe.

'Not a soul.'

'Perhaps it was someone who'd taken the wrong turning at the post office.' That was the postman.

'Wrong turning or not,' said Hepple severely, 'there was no call to be knocking Mrs Jenkins down.'

'And,' said Thorpe pertinently, 'having knocked her down to have driven on.'

*   *   *

It seemed to Henrietta Jenkins that she would never again be quite the same person as she had been before she stepped into the cold,

9

bare police mortuary.

A sad message, telephoned through a series of offices, had snatched her from the Greatorex Library where she had been working. A succession of kind hands had steered her into the hastily summoned taxi and put her onto the Berebury train. She had been barely aware of them. She vaguely remembered arriving at Berebury, where she got out more from force of habit than anything else. A police car had met her—she remembered that—and brought her to the police station.

Voices had indicated that there was no need for her to identify the body just now. Perhaps there were some other relatives?

No, Henrietta had told them. There was no one else. She was an only child and her father had been killed in the war.

Perhaps, then, there was someone close in Larking who would . . .

Henrietta had shaken her head.

Tomorrow then?

She had shaken her head again. Now.

Something like this was only possible if you didn't think about it. She heard herself say— very politely—'Now or never.'

She had followed a policeman down a long corridor. She didn't think she had ever seen a policeman without a helmet on—absurd the tricks one's mind played at a time like this.

He drew back a white sheet. Briefly. And

10

looked not at the still face lying there but at Henrietta's own live one.

She nodded speechlessly.

He laid the sheet back gently and led the way back to the world of the living. Henrietta was shivering now but not from cold. The policeman—she noticed for the first time that he was a sergeant—brought her a cup of tea. It was steaming hot and almost burnt her mouth but Henrietta drank it thirstily, gladly giving the hot liquid all her attention.

Even the sensation of pain, though, could not drive away the memory of the mortuary.

'It's the smell that upsets people,' said the police sergeant kindly. 'All that antiseptic.'

'It is a bit dank,' admitted Henrietta shakily. The detached, educated half of her mind noted how primitive it was of her to be so grateful for human company; but nothing would have taken her back into that other room again. Only if the body had been that of a stranger could she have borne that.

The sergeant busied himself about some papers on his desk while she drank. Presently she said, 'Sergeant, what happened?'

'The Larking postman found her lying in the road, miss. She'd been run over by a car on that last bad bend as you leave Larking village.'

'I know the place. Why?'

'Why was she knocked down? That we don't rightly know, miss. You see, the car didn't

11

stop.'

Henrietta stifled a rising wave of nausea.

'We'll pick him up, sooner or later, you'll see,' said the sergeant. 'Someone will have seen his number.'

Henrietta said dully, 'The number doesn't really matter to my mother or me now.'

'No, miss.' It seemed for a moment as if he was going to explain that it mattered to the police but instead he said carefully, 'Constable Hepple found her handbag—afterwards—and there was a letter from you inside it.'

'I always wrote on Sundays.'

'Yes, miss. People do that are away. Sunday's the day for that sort of thing . . .'

'I wish I'd had time to say something before . . .'

The sergeant offered what comfort he could. 'There's not a lot really needs saying, miss, not when it comes to the point. Families have said everything long ago, or else it's something that doesn't need saying.' He paused. 'What about tonight, miss?'

'I shall be all right.'

'We'll run you home to Larking, of course, but . . .'

'It's something I've got to get used to, isn't it?' she said. 'Being alone from now on.'

12

CHAPTER TWO

Police Constable Hepple of Down Martin was a conscientious man. First of all he measured the tyre mark in the grass and drew a plan. Then he borrowed an old sack from Bill Thorpe's tractor and covered the imprint against damage. After that he began a systematic search of the area.

He was rewarded with the discovery of Mrs Jenkins's handbag, which had been knocked out of her hand and flung into the long grass by the roadside. He took charge of this and continued his search but found nothing else. The letter inside from Henrietta having given her address he telephoned this and his report to his headquarters at Berebury, leaving to them the business of finding her and telling her the bad news.

He himself went back to the scene of the accident and took a plaster cast of the tyre mark. He then proceeded—as he would have said himself—to Boundary Cottage. He checked that it was safely locked—it was—and then went on to visit the other five cottages. Three of these were in a short row and two others and Boundary Cottage were detached, standing in their own not inconsiderable gardens.

There was no reply from Mulberry Cottage

which was Boundary Cottage's nearest neighbour—some people called Carter lived there—but all the occupants of the other cottages and of the two other farms besides the Thorpe's said the same thing. They had had no visitors the previous evening. They had heard and seen nothing.

Hepple went home and wrote out a second, slightly fuller report, and spent part of his afternoon in Larking village trying to establish who had been the last person to see Mrs Jenkins alive.

It was because of his careful checking over of Boundary Cottage that he was so surprised to have a telephone call from Henrietta the next morning.

'Someone's been in the house,' she said flatly.

'Have they, miss? What makes you think that?'

'In the front room . . .'

'Yes?' He had his notebook ready.

'There's a bureau. You know the sort of thing—you can write at it but it's not exactly a desk.'

'I know.'

'It's been broken into. Someone's prised the flap part open—they've damaged the wood.'

'When did you discover this, miss?'

Henrietta looked at her watch. It was just after ten o'clock in the morning. 'About ten minutes ago. I came straight out to ring you.'

14

'The damage, miss, you'd say it was someone trying to get inside without a key?'

'That's right.'

He hesitated. 'It couldn't have been your mother, miss? I mean, if she had lost her own key and needed to get in there quickly for something.'

'She'd never have spoilt it like this,' retorted Henrietta quickly. 'Besides, she wasn't the sort of person who lost keys.'

'Yes.' Hepple knew what she meant. His own impression of Mrs Jenkins was of a neat quiet lady. Law-abiding to a degree.

'Moreover,' went on Henrietta, 'if she had had to do something like that I'm sure she'd have told me in her letter.'

PC Hepple came back to the question of time.

'When?' repeated Henrietta vaguely. 'I don't know when.'

'Yesterday, miss. You came back yesterday.'

'That's right. They brought me home from Berebury in a police car afterwards . . .'

'About what time would that have been, miss?'

But time hadn't meant anything to Henrietta yesterday.

'It was dark. I don't know when exactly.'

'Was the bureau damaged then?' persisted Hepple.

'I don't know. I didn't go into the front room at all last night. I've just been in there

15

now . . .'

'The cottage was all locked up just gone twelve o'clock yesterday morning,' said Hepple, 'because I went along myself then to check. There were no signs of breaking and entering then, miss.'

'There aren't any now,' said Henrietta tersely. 'Just the bureau. That's the only thing that's wrong.'

With which, when he got there, PC Hepple was forced to agree.

'Windows and doors all all right,' he said. 'Unless they had a key, no one came in after I checked up yesterday morning.'

They went back to the front room and considered the bureau again. Henrietta pointed to a deep score in the old wood.

'My mother never did that. She'd have sent for a locksmith first.'

'Yes.' Now he could see the bureau, that was patently true. No one who owned a nice walnut piece like this would ever spoil it in that way just to get inside. 'What did she keep in there, miss, do you know?'

'All her papers,' said Henrietta promptly. 'Receipts, wireless licence—that sort of thing.'

'Money?'

'No, never. She didn't believe in keeping it in the house—especially a rather isolated one like this.'

'Jewellery?'

Henrietta shook her head. 'She didn't go in

16

for that either—she never wore anything that you could call jewellery. My father's medals, though. They were in there.'

Henrietta's gaze travelled from the bureau to the mantelpiece and a silver framed photograph of an army sergeant—and back to the bureau. 'They're in a little drawer at the side. I'll show you them if you like.'

'No,' said Hepple quickly. 'Don't you touch it, miss.'

She dropped her hands to her sides.

'Finger-prints,' said Hepple. 'It may not be worthwhile but you can't be sure until you've tried.'

'I hadn't thought of that . . .' Her voice trailed away.

'Now, miss, about last night.' Constable Hepple was nothing if not persistent.

'They brought me home in a police car sometime in the early evening I think it was. I didn't hear—about Mother until nearly lunch-time and it took me a while to get back to Berebury. Then I was there for quite a bit . . .'

'Yes, miss.'

'They didn't want to leave me alone the first night but I promised I'd go across to Mrs Carter if I wanted anything.'

'But,' agreed Hepple gently, 'the Carters are away. I called there this morning.'

'That's right. Only I didn't know that until I banged on her door and didn't get an answer. So I came back here.'

'Alone?'

'Yes.'

'You're sure you didn't come into this room?'

'Not until this morning.'

'You heard nothing in the night?'

'I didn't hear anyone levering the bureau open if that's what you mean. And I'm sure I would have done.'

They both regarded the splintered lock.

'Yes,' said Hepple, 'you would.'

'Besides which,' said Henrietta, heavy-eyed. 'I can't say that I slept much last night anyway.'

'No, miss,' the policeman was sympathetic. 'I don't suppose you did.'

'And this couldn't have been done quietly.'

'So,' said Hepple practically, 'that means that this was done before you got back yesterday evening, which was Wednesday, and after your mother left home for the last time— which was presumably some time on Tuesday.'

'That's right,' agreed Henrietta. 'If she'd had to do it, she'd have told me in a letter— and if she'd found it done I'm sure she would have told the police.

*   *   *

'Can't understand it at all, sir.' Police-Constable Hepple rang his headquarters at Berebury Station as soon as he left Boundary Cottage. He was put on to the Criminal

18

Investigation Department. 'Mind you, we don't know what's gone from the bureau—if anything. The young lady isn't familiar with its contents. Her mother always kept it locked.'

'Did she indeed?' said Detective Inspector Sloan.

'And there's no sign of forced entry anywhere.'

'Except the bureau.'

'That's right, sir.' Hepple paused significantly. 'I shouldn't have said myself it was the sort of place worth a burglary.'

'Really?' Sloan always listened to opinions of this sort.

'It's just one of Mr Hibbs's old cottages. Mind you, they keep it very nice. Always have done.'

'Who do?'

'Mrs Jenkins and Henrietta—that's the daughter. Of course, coming on top of the accident like this I thought I'd better report it special.'

'Quite right, Constable.'

'Seems a funny thing to happen.'

'It is,' said Sloan briefly. 'How far have they got with the accident?'

'Usual procedure with a fatal, sir. Traffic Division have asked all their cars to keep a look-out for a damaged vehicle, and all garages to report anything coming in for accident repair. I've got a decent cast of a nearside front tyre . . .'

'Size?'

'Five-ninety by fourteen.'

'Big,' said Sloan, just as Bill Thorpe had done.

'Yes, sir. They're asking for witnesses but they can't be sure of their timing until after the post-mortem. The local doctor put the time of death between six and nine o'clock on Tuesday evening, but I understand the pathologist is doing a post-mortem this morning.'

'We'll know a bit more after that,' agreed Sloan.

Wherein he was speaking more truthfully than he realised.

'Yes, sir,' said Hepple. 'They'll be able to fix an inquest date after that. I've warned the girl about it. But as to this other matter, sir . . .'

'The bureau?'

'It doesn't make sense to me. That house was all locked up when I went round it at twelve yesterday. I could swear no one broke in before then.'

Sloan twiddled a pencil. 'She could have gone out on Tuesday and forgotten to shut the door properly.'

'Ye-es,' said Hepple uneasily, 'but I don't think so. Careful sort of woman, I'd have said. Very.'

'When did she go out on Tuesday? Do we know that? And where had she been?'

'We don't know where she'd been, sir. No one seems to know that. Her daughter certainly doesn't. As to when, she caught the first bus into Berebury and came back on the last.'

'Not much help. She could have gone anywhere.'

'Yes, sir. And it meant the house was empty all day.'

'And all night.'

'All night?'

'She was lying in the road all night.'

'So she was,' said Hepple. 'I was forgetting. In fact, you could say the house was empty from first thing Tuesday morning until they brought the daughter from Berebury on Wednesday evening.'

'I wonder what was in the bureau?'

'I couldn't say, sir. She didn't keep money in there, nor jewellery. Nothing like that. Just papers, her daughter said.'

*   *   *

Detective Constable Crosby was young and brash and consciously represented the new element in the police force. The younger generation. He didn't usually volunteer to do anything. Which was why when Detective-Inspector Sloan heard him offering to take a set of papers back to Traffic Division he sat up and took notice.

'Nothing to do with us, sir,' Crosby said virtuously. 'Road Traffic Accident. Come to the CID by mistake, I reckon.'

'Then,' said Sloan pleasantly, 'you can reckon again.'

Crosby stared at the report. 'Woman, name of Grace Jenkins, run down by a car on a bad bend far end of Larking village.'

'That's right.'

'But Larking's miles away.'

'In the country,' agreed Sloan. 'Let's hope the natives are friendly.'

Sarcasm was wasted on Crosby. He continued reading aloud. 'Found by H. Ford, postman, believed to have been dead between ten and twelve hours, injuries consistent with vehicular impact?'

'That's the case. Read on. Especially PC Hepple's report of this morning.'

'Bureau in deceased's front room broken open. No signs of forced entry to the house.' Crosby sounded disappointed. 'That's not even breaking and entering, sir.'

'True.'

'I still don't see,' objected Crosby, 'what it's got to do with her being knocked down and killed.'

'Frankly, Crosby, neither do I.' Sloan put out his hand for the file. 'In fact there may be no connection whatsoever. In which case some of your valuable time will have been wasted.'

'Yes, sir.' Woodenly.

'That,' he added gravely, 'is a risk we shall have to take.'

22

Detective Inspector Sloan read the accident report again and thanked his lucky stars—not for the first time—that he didn't work in Traffic Division.

'Of all the nasty messes,' he mused aloud, 'I think a hit-and-run driver leaves the worst behind. No medical attention. No ambulance. No insurance.'

'And no prosecution,' said Crosby mordantly. He pointed to the report. 'Perhaps this character who hit her was drunk.'

'Perhaps.' Sloan got up from his desk. 'Though it was a bit early in the evening for that.'

'Perhaps *she* was drunk then,' suggested Crosby, undaunted.

Sloan shook his head. 'Hepple didn't suggest she was that sort of woman—quite the reverse in fact . . . A car, please, Crosby, and we shall venture into the outback at once.'

They didn't go quite straight away because the telephone on Sloan's desk started to ring.

'Berebury Hospital,' said a girl's voice. 'Can Inspector Sloan take a call from the Pathologist's Department, please?'

Crosby handed the receiver over to Sloan, who said, 'Speaking.'

'Dabbe here,' boomed a voice.

'Good morning, doctor,' said Sloan cautiously.

'I've been trying to talk to your Traffic Division about a woman I'm doing a p.m. on.'

'Yes?'

'They say she's your case now and you've got all the papers . . .'

'In a way,' agreed Sloan guardedly. He'd sort that out with Traffic afterwards.

'I've got her down,' said the pathologist, 'as Grace Edith Jenkins.'

'That's right. We're treating it as an RTA, doctor.'

'Road Traffic Accident she may be,' said the pathologist equably. 'I'll tell you about that later. That's not what I'm ringing about. The notes that came in with her say she was identified by her daughter.'

'That's right.'

'No, it isn't.'

Sloan picked up the file. 'Miss Henrietta Eleanor Leslie Jenkins said it was her mother.'

'Any doubt about the identification?'

'None that I've heard about, doctor.'

The pathologist grunted. 'She wasn't disfigured at all—there were no facial injuries to speak of.'

'No? Is it important, sir?'

'Either, Inspector, this girl . . .'

'Miss Jenkins.'

'Miss Jenkins has identified the wrong woman . . .'

'I don't think so,' objected Sloan, glancing swiftly through the notes in the file. 'The village postman and a neighbouring farmer's son called Thorpe put us onto her—to say

24

nothing of Constable Hepple. They all said it was Mrs Jenkins well before we got hold of her daughter.'

'That's just it,' said the pathologist.

'What is, sir?'

'She wasn't the daughter.'

'But . . .'

'This woman you've sent me may be Mrs Grace Edith Jenkins,' said Dabbe.

'She is.'

'I don't know about that,' went on the pathologist, 'but I can tell you one thing for certain and that's that she's never had any children.'

'Her daughter, doctor, said . . .'

'Not her daughter . . .'

Sloan paused and said carefully, 'Someone who told us she was Miss Henrietta Eleanor Leslie Jenkins then . . .'

'Ah,' said Dabbe, 'that's different.'

'She said she was prepared to swear in a Coroner's Court that this was the body of her mother, Mrs Grace Edith Jenkins, widow of Sergeant Cyril Jenkins of the East Calleshires.'

The pathologist sounded quite unimpressed.

'Very possibly,' he said. 'That's not really my concern but . . .'

'Yes?'

'You might take a note, Inspector, to the effect that I shall have to go to the same Coroner's Court and swear that, in my opinion, she—whoever she is—had certainly

25

never had any children and had very probably never been married either.'

CHAPTER THREE

'Have you turned over two pages or something, Sloan?'

The Superintendent of Police in Berebury glared across his desk at the Head of Criminal Investigation Department. It was a very small department, all matters of great moment being referred to the Calleshire County Constabulary Headquarters in Calleford.

'No, sir. The girl positively identified the woman as her mother and Dr Dabbe, the pathologist, says the woman had never had any children.'

'How does he know?' Truculently.

'I couldn't begin to say, sir,' said Sloan faintly. The Superintendent's first reaction was always the true English one of challenging the expert. 'But he was quite definite about it.'

'He always is.'

'Yes, sir.' Sloan coughed. 'There are really three matters ...'

Superintendent Leeyes grunted discouragingly.

'First of all a woman is knocked down and killed on Tuesday evening not far from her home.' Sloan stopped and amended this. 'Not far from what we believe is her home. At some stage before or after this but before Wednesday evening someone lets himself into her house with a key but doesn't have a key to the bureau so breaks it open . . .'

'Why?'

'We don't know yet, sir. Thirdly . . .'

'Well?'

'The woman isn't the mother of the girl who identified her as her mother.'

'It's not difficult,' said Leeyes loftily. 'She's probably the father's bastard.'

Sloan ignored this and said conversationally, 'Mrs Jenkins seems to have been a very unusual woman, sir.'

'You can say that again,' said the Superintendent. 'I've never heard of unnatural childbirth before.'

'She managed,' Sloan was still struggling to keep the tone at an academic level, 'she managed to keep her private affairs private in a small village like Larking.'

'I'll admit that takes some doing. Did she have a record then?'

'I don't know, sir, yet, but that's not quite the same thing as a secret.'

'No? Perhaps, Sloan, I've been in the Force too long . . .'

'I think this secret must have been of a matrimonial nature.'

The Superintendent brightened at once. 'Then perhaps it was Mr Jenkins who had the record.'

'I'll check on that naturally, sir, but there is another possibility.'

'There are lots of possibilities.'

'Yes, sir.'

'Not all of them to do with us.'

'No, sir. This could well be just a family matter.'

'Most of our cases,' the Superintendent reminded him tartly, doing one of his famous smart verbal about-turns, 'are family matters.'

'Yes, sir.' He paused. 'Constable Hepple doesn't know anything about them not being mother and daughter and he's been living out that way for donkey's years.'

'A good man, Hepple,' conceded Leeyes. 'Knows all the gossip. If there's much crime in the south of Calleshire he never tells us.'

This might not have been Her Majesty's Inspector of Constabulary's view of what constituted a good policeman but the Superintendent was not a man who looked for work.

'What are you going to do about it?' he asked Sloan.

'See the girl for a start—and the bureau.'

'She could be lying.' Leeyes tapped Traffic Division's file. 'According to Dr Dabbe she is.'

'Her mother could have lied to her . . .'

'A by-blow of the father's,' repeated the Superintendent firmly, 'for sure, brought up as her own. Some women will swallow anything.'

28

'Perhaps,' said Sloan cautiously. 'But just suppose she isn't Grace Edith Jenkins?'

Superintendent Leeyes looked quite attentive at last. 'I don't believe we've had a case of personation in the county for all of twenty years.'

*   *   *

Young Thorpe had called at Boundary Cottage to see if Henrietta needed anything, and to say how sorry he was.

'It is nice of you, Bill,' she said sincerely, 'but I'm quite all right.'

He stood awkwardly in the doorway, almost filling it with his square shoulders. He wasn't all that young either but being Mr Thorpe of Shire Oak Farm's son he was destined to be known as young Thorpe for many years yet.

'I liked your mother, you know,' he said, 'in spite of everything.'

'I know you did, Bill,' Henrietta said quickly.

'She was probably right to make us wait. First I was away at the Agricultural College and then with her being so keen on your going away too.'

Henrietta nodded. 'She really minded about that, didn't she?'

'Some people just feel that way about education,' said Bill Thorpe seriously. 'My father's the same. He couldn't go to college

29

himself but he made me. He's right, I suppose. You learn—well, it's not exactly how much you learn but the reasons behind things.'

'And it wasn't very long, was it?'

He smiled wanly. 'It seemed a long time.'

'You never wrote.'

'Neither did you,' returned Bill.

'We promised not to. I thought it might make things easier.'

'Did it?'

Henrietta shook her head. 'No.'

'Nor for me.' He looked at her for a minute, then, 'Mother said to come to the farm to sleep if you wanted.'

'Will you say thank you? There's nothing I'd like more but,' she grimaced, 'I think if I once didn't stay here on my own I'd never get back to doing it again. She'll understand, I know.'

Thorpe nodded. 'We're a bit out of the way, too, at the farm. There'll be a lot to be done here I expect.'

'It's not that, but,' she pushed her hair back vaguely, 'there seem to be people coming all the time. The Rector's coming down to talk to me about the funeral and Mr Hepple said he'd be back again about the inquest.' She gave a shaky half-laugh. 'I'd no idea dying was such a—well—complicated business.'

'No,' agreed Thorpe soberly. He allowed a decent interval to elapse before he said, 'Any news of the car?'

'What car—oh, that car? No, Bill, they

haven't said anything to me about it yet.'

*   *   *

Henrietta thought that Inspector Sloan and Constable Crosby had come from the Berebury CID solely to examine her mother's bureau for finger-prints.

'It's in the front room,' she said, leading the way. 'I haven't touched it.'

Sloan obligingly directed Crosby to perform this routine procedure while he talked to Henrietta.

'Nothing missing from the rest of the house, miss?'

'Not that I know of, Inspector. It all looks all right to me.' She paused. 'It's such an odd thing to happen, isn't it?'

'Yes,' said Sloan simply.

'I mean, why should someone want to break in here . . .'

'Not break in, miss. PC Hepple said all the doors and windows were intact. He found the place quite well locked up really. Whoever got in here came in by the door. The front door.'

('The back one's bolted as well as the Tower of London,' was what Hepple had said.)

'The front door,' he repeated.

'That's worse,' said Henrietta.

'Your mother, miss, would she have left a key with anyone?'

'No.' Henrietta considered this. 'I'm sure

31

she wouldn't. Besides there were only two keys. There was one in her handbag and one hanging on a hook in the kitchen. That's the one I use when I'm at home.'

'I see.'

Henrietta shivered suddenly. 'I don't like to think of someone coming in here . . .'

'No, miss.'

'. . . with a key.'

Sloan wasn't exactly enamoured of the idea either. It left the girl in the state that insurance companies called being 'at risk.'

'Now, miss, I think we can open the bureau.'

Crosby had finished his dusting operations. He stook back and said briefly, 'Gloves.'

Sloan was not surprised.

'Was it usually kept locked?' he asked Henrietta.

'Always.'

'Are you familiar with its contents?'

'Not really. My mother kept her papers there. I couldn't say if they are all there or not.'

Sloan eased back the flap. Everything was neatly pigeonholed. Either no one had been through the bureau or they had done it conscious that they would be undisturbed. Sloan pulled out the first bundle of papers.

'Housekeeping accounts,' he said, glancing rapidly through them. Grace Jenkins and her alleged daughter had lived modestly enough.

'That's right,' said Henrietta. 'You'll find

her cheque-book there too.'

Sloan took a quick look at the bank's name for future reference. The account was at a Berebury branch. He put the tidily docketed receipts back and took out the next bundle. It brought an immediate flush to Henrietta's cheeks.

'I'd no idea she kept those.'

Sloan looked down at a schoolgirl's writing.

'My letters to her,' she said in a choked voice, 'and my school reports.'

If this was acting, thought Sloan, it was good acting.

'Mothers do.' He chose his words carefully. 'Part of the treasury of parenthood, you might say. By the way, where did you go to school?'

'Here in the village first, then Berebury High.'

Sloan put the infant Henrietta's literary efforts back in their place and took out the next bundle.

'These seem to be about the cottage.' He turned over a number of letters. 'Fire insurance, rating assessment and so forth.'

Sloan put them back but not before noting that all were quite definitely in the name of Mrs G. E. Jenkins.

'Boundary Cottage,' he said. 'Did it belong to your mo—to Mrs Jenkins?'

'No,' Henrietta shook her head. 'To Mr Hibbs at The Hall. It's the last of the cottages on his estate. That's why it's called Boundary

Cottage.'

'Can you think of any reason why anyone would want to break in here?'

She shook her head again. 'I don't think she kept anything valuable there. That's why I can't understand anyone wanting to go through it. There wasn't anything to steal . . .'

'It doesn't look,' he said cautiously, 'as if, in fact, anything has been stolen.'

She reached over and pointed out a little drawer. 'If you would just look inside that, Inspector . . . thank you. Ah, they're all right. My father's medals.'

It was the opening Sloan was looking for.

'I'll need a note of his full name, miss, for the inquest.'

'Sergeant Cyril Edgar Jenkins.'

'And your mother's maiden name?'

'Wright,' said Henrietta unhesitatingly.

'Thank you. That's his photograph, I take it?'

'It is.' Henrietta handed it down from the mantelpiece and gave it to Sloan. 'He was in the East Calleshires.'

'That's unusual, isn't it, miss? I mean, they're mostly West Calleshires in these parts.'

'He came from East Calleshire,' she said.

'I see.' Sloan studied the picture of a fair-haired man in soldier's uniform and glanced back at Henrietta's darker colouring.

'I was more like my mother to look at,' she said, correctly interpreting his glance. 'The

34

same colour hair . . .'

But Mrs Jenkins was not her mother. Dr Dabbe had said so.

'Really, miss?' said Sloan aloud. 'Now, you wouldn't have a photograph of her by any chance?'

'In my bedroom. I'll fetch it.'

'A pretty kettle of fish,' observed Sloan gravely to Crosby the minute she was out of earshot.

'Someone's been through that bureau with a toothcomb, sir,' said Crosby. 'Glove prints everywhere.'

'Wonder what they wanted?'

'Search me.' Crosby ran his fingers in behind pigeon-holes, pressing here and pulling there. 'Nothing to suggest a secret drawer.'

'That's something to be thankful for anyway . . . Ah, there you are, miss, thank you.'

Henrietta handed him a snapshot in a leather frame—quite a different matter from the studio portrait that had stood on the mantelpiece.

'It's not a very good one but it's the only one I've got.'

Sloan held the snap in front of him. It was of an ordinary middle-aged woman, taken standing outside the back door of the cottage. She had on a simple cotton frock and had obviously been prevailed upon to come out of the kitchen to be photographed. She was smiling in a protesting sort of way at the

35

camera.

'I was lucky to have one of her to show you,' said Henrietta. The sight of the picture had brought a quaver into her voice which she strove to conceal from the two policemen. 'She didn't like having her photograph taken.'

'Didn't she indeed?'

'But I had a university friend to stay for a few days the summer before last and she had a camera with her.'

'Do you mean to say, miss, that this is the only photograph of your mother extant?'

She frowned. 'I think so. Angela—that was her name—sent it to us when she got home.'

Inspector Sloan stood the two photographs side by side, the formal silver-framed studio study and the quick amateur snapshot.

'On my left, a sergeant in the East Calleshire Regiment called Cyril Edgar Jenkins . . .'

'My father,' said Henrietta.

'Aged about—what would you say?'

'He was thirty-one,' supplied Henrietta. 'Is it important?'

'And on my right a middle-aged woman called Grace Edith Jenkins . . .'

'My mother,' said Henrietta.

There was a short silence. Henrietta looked first at one policeman and then at the other.

Sloan avoided her clear gaze and said, 'Can you remember anything before Larking?'

'No, I can't.' She looked at him curiously

36

but she answered his question. 'I've lived here ever since I can remember. In Boundary Cottage. With my mother.'

'And you don't remember your father at all?'

'No. He was killed soon after I was born.'

'What do you know about him?'

'Him?'

'Yes, miss. I'll explain in a minute.'

She hesitated. She had an image of her father in her mind, always had had and it was compounded of many things: the words of her mother, the photograph in the drawing-room the conception of any soldier, of all soldiers, killed in battle—but it wasn't something easily put into words.

'He wasn't afraid,' she said awkwardly.

'I realise that.' They didn't award medals for cowardice. 'But what do you know about him as a person? What was his occupation, for instance?'

'He worked on a farm.'

'Did he own it?' Property owners as a class of person were easy to trace, popular with the police.

'I don't think so. He was the farm bailiff for someone.' She frowned. 'His father had a small farm though. It wasn't really big enough for my father to work as well—that's why he worked for someone else.'

'Whereabouts?'

'Somewhere on the other side of Calleshire.

37

I'm not sure exactly where.'

'So that is where your mother came from to Larking?'

'From that direction somewhere, I suppose. I don't know exactly. She said he—my father, that is—had moved about a bit getting experience. He would have had to run his father's farm one day on his own and he needed to learn.'

'I see.' He gave her a quick grin. 'So on Saturday nights, miss, you—er—support the East Callies?'

She responded with a faint smile. The regimental rivalry between the East and West Calleshires was famous. 'They get on very well without my help. The West Callies have lost their mascot twice already this year.'

'Have they indeed? Vulnerable things, mascots. Now this farm of your—er—grandfather's—do you know where that was?'

'It was called Holly Tree Farm, I know,' said Henrietta promptly, 'because I remember my mother telling me there was a very old holly tree there that my grandfather wouldn't have cut down even though it was just in front of the house and made the rooms very dark. He used to say you can't have a Holly Tree Farm without a holly tree.'

'A very proper attitude,' agreed Sloan stoutly. 'Did you ever go there?'

'Not that I can remember. I think he died when I was quite young.'

'But your mother used to talk about the farm?'

'Oh, yes, a lot. She grew up near there too.'

'And so she had known your father all her life?'

Henrietta nodded. 'Certainly since they were children. She used to tell me a lot about him when he was a little boy. But, Inspector, I don't see what this has got to do with my mother's death.'

'No, miss, I don't suppose you do.' Sloan paused judiciously. 'It's not easy to say this, miss, and if it weren't a matter of you having to give formal evidence of identification at the inquest it might not even be something we need to take cognisance of.'

'What might not be?' Henrietta looked quite mystified.

'This Cyril Jenkins . . .'

'My father?'

'Had he been married twice by any chance?'

'Not that I know of. Why?'

'Or Grace Jenkins? Had she been married to anyone else besides Cyril Jenkins?'

A slow flush mounted Henrietta's cheeks. 'No, Inspector, not to my knowledge.'

Like a cat picking its way over a wet path Sloan said delicately, 'There is a possibility that your name may not be Jenkins.'

'Not Jenkins?'

'Not Jenkins.'

'I may be being very stupid,' said Henrietta,

'but I don't see why not.'

'It was Dr Dabbe.'

'Dr Dabbe?'

'The pathologist, miss, from the hospital. He conducted a post-mortem examination on the body of the woman who was knocked down.'

'That's right.' She nodded. 'My mother.'

'No, miss.'

Henrietta sat down suddenly. 'I came into the police station on Wednesday—yesterday, that was—when I got back. They asked me to look at her. I signed something. There was a sergeant there—he'll tell you.' She screwed up her face at the recollection. 'There wasn't any doubt. I wish there had been. It was her. Her face, her clothes, her handbag. I've never seen anyone dead before but I was absolutely certain . . .'

Sloan put up a hand to stem the memory. 'It's not quite that, miss . . .' He couldn't tell if she knew nothing at all or if she knew a great deal more than he did. It was impossible to know.

She pushed a strand of hair away from her face and said very quietly, 'Well, what exactly is it, then?'

'This woman whom you identified yesterday as Mrs Grace Edith Jenkins . . .'

'Yes?'

Sloan didn't hurry to go on. He felt oddly embarrassed. This wasn't the sort of subject you discussed with young girls. He didn't often

40

wish work onto the women members of the Force but perhaps this might have been one of the times when . . .

'I'm sorry to have to tell you, miss, that the pathologist says, she never had any children.'

A blush flamed up Henrietta's pale face. She tried to speak but for a moment no sound came. Then she managed a shaky little laugh. 'I'm afraid there must have been some terrible mistake, Inspector . . .'

Sloan shook his head.

'A mix-up at the hospital, perhaps,' she went on, heedless of his denial. 'It happens with babies sometimes, doesn't it? Perhaps it's the same sometimes in—in other places . . .'

'No, miss . . .'

She took a deep breath. 'That was my mother I saw yesterday. Beyond any doubt.'

The doubt in Sloan's mind, because he was a policeman paid to doubt, was whether the girl was party to this knowledge about Grace Jenkins. He didn't let it alter his behaviour.

'I fear,' gently, 'that the pathologist is equally adamant that the subject of his examination had never borne a child.'

He saw the blush on the face of the girl in front of him fade away to nothing as she suddenly went very very pale.

'But . . .' Henrietta's world seemed suddenly to have no fixed points at all. She struggled to think and to speak logically. 'But who am I then?'

CHAPTER FOUR

'Where do we go from here, sir?'

'That you may well ask, Crosby.' Sloan was irritable and preoccupied as they walked away from Boundary Cottage. 'All we've got so far is a girl who isn't who she thinks she is, the body of a woman who probably wasn't what she said she was and two photographs.'

'Yes, sir.' Crosby closed the gate behind them.

'Added to which we're leaving an unprotected girl, who has just been subjected to a great emotional shock, alone in a relatively isolated house to which we strongly suspect someone has already gained admittance with a key.'

'She could go to friends. There must be someone near who would have her.'

'I don't doubt that, but it would be most unwise of her to go to them.'

'Unwise, sir?'

'Unwise, Crosby. If we advise it, and she goes, she might have difficulty in regaining possession of her mother's—of Mrs Jenkins's—belongings.'

'I hadn't thought about that, sir.' There was a distinct pause while Crosby did think about it, then, 'Regaining them from whom, sir?'

'I don't know.'

'I see sir.' He didn't, in fact, see anything at all but thought it prudent not to say so.

'Have you thought that after this she may well not be in a position to prove her title to the cottage tenancy?'

'No, sir.' Crosby digested this in silence. Then, 'A sort of Tichborne Claimant in reverse, you might say, sir.'

'That's it,' agreed Sloan. He knew Crosby, who was ambitious for promotion, had recently taken to looking up old cases. He stood for a moment beside the police car and then said, 'A landlord usually knows a tenant as well as anyone after a while. Drive to The Hall, Crosby.'

The Hall lay between the village and Boundary Cottage, to the south of the church. Whereas the Rectory was Georgian, the Hall was older. It was quite small, but perfectly proportioned.

'That's it,' observed Sloan with satisfaction. 'They had a bit about it in one of those magazines last year. My wife showed it to me. Late Tudor.'

'Make a nice Rest Home for tired constables,' said Crosby.

James Hibbs saw them in his study. He was a well-built man in tweeds. His hair was black running to grey and Sloan put his age at about fifty-five. As they went in, two aristocratic gun dogs looked the two policemen over, decided they were not fair game and settled back

43

disdainfully on the hearth.

'Shocking business,' agreed Hibbs. 'Don't like to think of something like that happening on your own doorstep, do you?'

'No, sir.'

'Any news of the fellow who did it?'

'Not yet, sir.'

'All in good time, I suppose.' He sighed. 'A good woman. Brought that girl up very well considering.'

'Considering what, sir?'

Hibbs waved a hand. 'That she'd had to do it on her own. No father, you know. Just her pension.'

'Had you known her long?'

'Couldn't say I really knew her at all. She wasn't that sort of a woman. But she'd been here quite a while.' He looked curiously at Sloan. 'She came to Larking during the war. Couldn't tell you exactly when. Is it important?'

'No, sir. What we're trying to trace are some other relatives besides the girl.'

'Oh, I see. Yes, I suppose she's still under age. Must be, of course, now I come to think of it.'

'Why?'

'The Thorpe boy wanted to marry Henrietta and Mrs Jenkins said no.'

'Really, sir? On what grounds?'

'Age. The girl wasn't twenty-one at the time and still at university. Another year to go, then.'

Sloan's gaze travelled upwards over the fireplace. An old oar, smoke-darkened, rested above it. A long time ago James Hibbs had rowed for his college.

'Nice lad,' remarked Hibbs. 'Can't think why she opposed it.'

'To go back a bit further, sir . . .'

'Yes?'

'When she came here. Do you know where it was from?'

Hibbs frowned. 'I had an idea it was East Calleshire somewhere, but I couldn't be certain. I'd plenty of empty cottages on my hands at the time and old White would have been glad enough to get a tenant of any sort.'

'Old White?'

'My agent at the time. Dead now, of course. He fixed it all up. I was only here intermittently. On leave.'

'I see.'

'Never thought we'd get anyone to live in Boundary Cottage after old Miss Potter died. Too far out.'

'And how did you get Mrs Jenkins?'

Hibbs shrugged his shoulders. 'I couldn't tell you, Inspector, not at this distance of time. White might have advertised it but I doubt it. Sending good money after bad in those days.'

'Not now, sir.'

'Good Lord, no. I could have sold it a dozen times since then if it had been empty. Sort of place people see on a Sunday afternoon drive in summertime and think they'd like to live in.'

'Yes.' Sloan looked reflectively round the study. 'You wouldn't happen to have any records about this tenancy still, would you, sir?'

Hibbs considered this. 'It's worth a look, I suppose. Old White was one of the old school. Neatest man I ever knew. Care to walk across to the Estate Office?'

Hibbs introduced them to the young man who was working there, called Threlkeld.

'Boundary Cottage, Mr Hibbs?' Threlkeld stepped across to a filing cabinet. In the background Sloan could hear the low hum of a milking-machine plant. The Hall was being run on very business-like lines. A file was produced. 'What was it you wished to see?'

'The tenancy agreement, please.'

Sloan watched him turn back the contents of the file. On top were details of the Rural District Council's Main Drainage connections, then, under a date for a few years earlier an estimate for repairs to the roof, Schedule 'A' forms galore, more estimates, much smaller ones as they went back through the years.

Sloan almost whistled aloud when he saw the figure for the rent.

'Not a lot, is it?' said Hibbs ruefully. 'That's the Rent Restriction Act for you.'

Threlkeld went on turning back the pages. Everything was in date order. Suddenly the

46

handwriting changed to an old-fashioned copperplate.

'Old White,' said Hibbs. 'Wrote a beautiful fist.'

Threlkeld paused. 'Here we are, Mr Hibbs. Miss Potter died in the December.'

'Pneumonia,' said Hibbs. 'I can remember that much.'

'The new tenant,' went on Threlkeld, 'took possession at the end of May. It was empty in between. You apparently signed an all-repairs lease . . .'

'For my sins,' groaned Hibbs.

'. . . and it was accepted by her solicitors on behalf of their client in this letter, dated May 28th.'

'Oh,' said Sloan.

'It *was* East Calleshire then,' said Hibbs. 'I had an idea it was. Look, they were Calleford solicitors.'

Sloan leaned over and read the address aloud. 'Waind, Arbican and Waind, Ox Lane, Calleford.'

Acting on behalf of their client, Mrs G. E. Jenkins, they had advised her to accept Mr Hibbs's offer of Boundary Cottage, Larking, at the rent as stated.

'You don't remember her at all before this date, sir?'

Hibbs shook his head. 'No. She came quite out of the blue. Old White probably thought that was a fair enough rent at the time and better than nothing.'

'He was wrong,' said Threlkeld. 'No rent at all would have been better.'

Hibbs turned. 'It's easy to be wise after the event, Threlkeld. Besides, in those days one did give some consideration to widows and orphans.'

Hibbs agreed readily enough to Sloan borrowing the letter and they took it back to Berebury with them.

*   *   *

Henrietta waited until Sloan and Crosby had gone.

She made herself stay sitting down in the front room until she heard the police car draw away. Then she slipped on a coat and left the house.

It was fresher outside. There was a March wind blowing and she felt more free than in the confined atmosphere of the house. Boundary Cottage had suddenly become much too small for her—there hardly seemed air enough inside for her to breathe.

She didn't go along the road but through the orchard behind the cottage and then along the old footpath. It brought her out near the church. Across the green from the church was the Rectory.

She went up to the door. It was half-open. Somewhere beyond in the wide hall someone was counting aloud.

'Four, five . . .'

She knocked on the door.

'Who is it?' called a woman's voice.

'I d . . . don't know,' said Henrietta miserably.

'Well, come in whoever it is—oh, it's you Henrietta. Come in, dear, and just hold that for me, will you, while I finish these. I won't be a minute.' A short, stout woman pushed a pile of freshly laundered surplices into Henrietta's hands. 'Now, where was I?'

'Five.'

'Six, seven, eight—what that Callows boy does with his, I can't think—nine, ten. That's the lot, thank goodness.' She took the bundle back again. 'Edward can take them across with him later. Now, come along in by the fire. You look frozen.'

'I'm not cold. Just a bit shaky, that's all.'

'I'm not surprised,' retorted Mrs Meyton. 'Losing your poor mother like that. A terrible shock. The Rector was coming down to see you this afternoon—didn't you get his message?'

'Yes. Yes, I did.' Henrietta drew in a deep breath. 'Mrs Meyton . . .'

'Yes, dear?'

'I want you to tell me something.'

'What's that?'

'Do you remember my mother and me coming here?'

Mrs Meyton nodded vigorously. 'Yes, dear. It was just before the war ended.'

'Did we come together?'

'Did you come together?' She smiled. 'Of course you did. You were only a very tiny baby, you know. I remember it quite well. Such a sad little family.'

'My father . . .'

Here Mrs Meyton shook her head. 'No, it was just after he was killed. I never met him.'

'But,' urgently, 'you do remember us coming together?'

'Certainly. Boundary Cottage had been empty for a long time—since old Miss Potter died, in fact—and I remember how glad we were that someone was going to live in it after all.' Mrs Meyton raised her eyebrows heavenwards. 'A rare old state it was in, I can tell you, but your mother soon got to work on it and she had it as right as ninepence in next to no time—garden and all.'

'She liked things just so . . .'

Mrs Meyton wasn't listening. 'How the years do go by. It hardly seems the other day but it must be all of twenty years . . .'

'Twenty-one,' said Henrietta. 'I'll be twenty-one next month.'

'I suppose you will.' Mrs Meyton regarded the passing years with disfavour. 'I don't know where the time goes. And the older you get the more quickly it passes.'

'Baptism,' said Henrietta suddenly.

'What about it, dear?'

'Was I christened here in Larking?'

But here Mrs Meyton's parochial memory failed her. She frowned hard. 'Now, I would have to think about that. Is it important? Edward would know. At least,' she added loyally, 'he could look it up in the register.'

Memory was not one of the Rector's strong points.

'Do you think he would? You see,' Henrietta swallowed hard, 'you see, the police have just told me that Grace Jenkins wasn't my mother after all.'

Mrs Meyton looked disbelieving. 'Not your mother?'

'That's what they said.'

'But,' said Mrs Meyton in a perplexed voice, 'if she wasn't, who was?'

'That's what I'd like to know.' There was a catch in Henrietta's voice as she said, 'I expect I'm illegitimate.'

'Nonsense.' Mrs Meyton shook her head. There were thirty years of being a clergyman's wife behind her when she said, 'Your mother wasn't the sort of woman to have an illegitimate baby.'

'She hadn't ever had any children,' said Henrietta bleakly, 'and she wasn't my mother, so it doesn't apply.'

'And I shouldn't have said myself,' went on Mrs Meyton, 'that she was the sort of woman to say she'd had a baby if it wasn't hers.'

'Neither would I,' agreed Henrietta promptly. 'That's the funny thing . . .'

'But if she did, I expect she had a good reason. They must have adopted you.'

'I hadn't thought of that.'

'A cup of tea,' said Mrs Meyton decisively, 'that's what we both need.'

Ten minutes later Henrietta put her cup down with a clatter. 'I've just thought of something . . .'

'What's that, dear?'

'How do I know I'll be twenty-one in April?'

'Because . . .' Mrs Meyton's voice trailed away. 'Oh, I see what you mean.' Then, 'A birth certificate, dear. You must have a birth certificate. Everyone does.'

'Do they? I've never seen mine.'

'You'll have one somewhere. You'll see. Your mother will have kept it in a safe place for sure.'

'The bureau . . .' cried Henrietta.

'That's right,' said Mrs Meyton comfortably.

'It's not right,' retorted Henrietta. 'Someone broke in to the bureau on Tuesday.'

'Oh, dear.'

'And there's certainly no birth certificate in there now . . .'

'A copy,' said Mrs Meyton gamely. 'You can send for one from Somerset House.'

'But don't you see,' cried Henrietta in despair, 'if she wasn't my mother I don't know what name to ask for.'

CHAPTER FIVE

'Crosby . . .'

'Sir?' Crosby had one ear glued to the telephone receiver but he listened to Sloan with the other.

'You tell me why a woman brings up a child as her own when it isn't.'

'Adopted, sir, that's all.'

'Why?'

'Why adopt, sir? I couldn't say, sir. Seems quite unnecessary to me. Asking for trouble.'

'Why adopt when she did,' said Sloan. 'That's what I want to know.'

'When?' echoed Crosby.

'The middle of a war, that's when. With her husband on active service.'

'Do we know that, sir, for sure?'

'We don't know anything for sure,' Sloan reminded him with some acerbity, 'except that Dr Dabbe swears that this Grace Edith Jenkins never had any children.' He paused. 'We know one or two odd things, of course.'

'The bureau?'

'The bureau. Someone broke into that for a reason.'

'They found what they were looking for . . .'

'Yes, I think they did. Something else that's odd, Crosby . . .'

Crosby thought for a moment. 'Odd that

they didn't have to break into the house. Just the bureau.'

'Very odd, that.'

'Yes, sir.' Crosby waved his free hand. 'Dr Dabbe is coming on the line from the hospital now, sir.'

Sloan took the receiver.

'This road traffic accident you sent me, Sloan, one Grace Edith Jenkins . . .'

'Yes, doctor?'

'I confirm the time of death. Between six and nine o'clock on Tuesday evening. Nearer nine than six.'

'Thank you.' Sloan started to write.

'She was aged about fifty-five,' continued the pathologist.

'Forty-five, I think it was, doctor.' Sloan turned back the pages of the file. 'Yes. Her daughter said she was forty-five. Forty-six next birthday.'

'And I,' said Dr Dabbe mildly, 'said she was about fifty-five.'

Sloan made his first significant note.

'She had also had her hair dyed fairly recently.'

'Oh?' said Sloan.

'From—er—blonde to brunette.'

'Had she indeed?' The pathologist never missed anything. 'I should say she had been hit from behind by a car that was travelling pretty fast. The main injury was a ruptured aorta and she would have died very quickly from it.'

'Outright?'

'In my opinion, yes.'

That, at least, was something to be thankful for.

'I should say the car wheel went right over her, also rupturing the spleen. There are plenty of surface abrasions . . .'

'I'm not surprised.'

'Both ante-mortem and post-mortem.'

'Post-mortem?'

'There was also a post-mortem fracture of the right femur,' said the pathologist.

Sloan said, 'I'm sorry to hear that,'

'I fear,' said Dr Dabbe, 'that these injuries are consistent with her having been run over by a heavy vehicle twice.'

'Two successive cars?' asked Sloan hopefully.

The pathologist sounded cautious. 'I'd have to see the plan of how she was lying but I'd have said she was definitely hit from behind the first time.'

'That's what the constable in attendance thought.'

'And from the opposite direction the second time.'

'Nasty.'

'Yes . . .'

Sloan replaced the receiver and looked out of the window. 'A car, Crosby, and quickly. I want to get back to Larking before the light goes. And get on to Hepple and tell him to meet us at the scene of the accident.'

*　　　*　　　*

Henrietta was still at the Rectory when the Rector returned. He wasn't altogether surprised when his wife told him that Henrietta was not Grace Jenkins's daughter.

'That explains something that always puzzled me,' he said.

Henrietta looked up quickly. 'What was that?'

'Why she came to Larking in the first place. As far as I could discover she had no links here at all. None whatsoever.' Mr Meyton was a spare, grey-haired scholarly man, a keen student of military history, and the direct opposite of his tubby cheerful wife. 'If I remember correctly you both arrived out of the blue so to speak. And no one could call Boundary Cottage the ideal situation for an unprotected woman and child in wartime.'

Henrietta blinked. 'I hadn't thought of that . . .'

'If she was deliberately looking for somewhere lonely . . .'

'Nowhere better,' agreed Henrietta. 'I just thought she liked the country.'

'It occurred to me at the time she had set out to cut herself off,' said Mr Meyton. 'Some people do. A great mistake, of course, and I always advise against it.'

'Now we know why,' said Henrietta.

'Perhaps.'

'She wanted everyone to think I was hers.'

'She probably didn't want you to know you weren't,' said Mr Meyton mildly. 'Which is something quite different.'

'But why on earth not?' demanded Henrietta. 'Lots of children are adopted these days.'

'True.' The Rector hesitated. 'There are other possibilities, of course.'

'I'm just beginning to work them out,' dryly.

'She might have had you by a previous marriage.'

'No. It wasn't that.'

'Or even—er—outside marriage.'

'Nor that,' said Henrietta tonelessly. 'The police said so. She wasn't anybody's mother—ever.'

'I see. There will be reasons, you know.'

She sighed. 'I could have understood any of those things but this just doesn't make sense.'

'It is an unusual situation.' Mr Meyton gave the impression of choosing his words with care.

'Grace Jenkins brought me up as a daughter,' said Henrietta defiantly, 'whatever anyone says.'

'Quite so.'

'And I swear no one could have been kinder . . .'

'No.' He said tentatively, 'Perhaps—had you

thought—most likely of all, I suppose—that you were a child of your father's by a previous marriage of his.'

Mrs Meyton, who had been sitting by, worried and concerned, put in: 'That would explain everything, dear, wouldn't it?'

'I had wondered about that,' said Henrietta.

The Rector stirred his tea. 'It is a distinct possibility.'

Henrietta stared into the fire. 'That would make me her stepdaughter.'

'Yes.' He coughed. 'It might also account for the strange fact that after all he was dead by then and she wouldn't have wanted you to feel insecure, so she didn't tell you.'

'She didn't,' said Henrietta vigorously, 'behave like a stepmother.'

'That's a fiction, you know,' retorted the Rector. 'You've been reading too many books.'

Henrietta managed a tremulous smile, and said again, 'Grace Jenkins brought me up as a daughter. I know she loved me . . .'

'Of course she did,' insisted Mrs Meyton.

'Perhaps that's the wrong word,' said Henrietta slowly. 'It was more than that. I always felt . . .' She looked from one of them to the other, struggling to find a word that would convey intangible meaning: '. . . well, cherished, if you know what I mean.'

'Of course I do,' said Mrs Meyton briskly. 'And you were. Always.'

'It wasn't only that. She made great

sacrifices so that I could go away to university. We had to be very careful, you know, with money.' She pushed her hair back from her face and said, 'She wouldn't have done that for just anybody, would she?'

What could have been a small smile twitched at the corners of the Rector's lips but he said gravely enough, 'I think we can accept that, whoever you are, you aren't—er—just anybody.'

'But am I even Henrietta?'

'Henrietta?'

'Henrietta Eleanor Leslie—those are my Christian names . . .'

'Well?'

'I thought I was my mother's daughter until this morning.'

'You're looking for proof that . . .'

'That at least I'm Henrietta.'

'If you had been baptised here . . .'

'I wasn't then?'

The Rector shook his head. 'No. Your mother . . .'

'She wasn't my mother.'

'I'm sorry.' He bowed his head. 'I was forgetting. It isn't easy to remember . . .'

'No.' Very ironically.

'Mrs Jenkins told me you were already baptised.'

He did remember then. Aloud Henrietta said, 'That's why the bureau was broken into. I can see that now.'

'You think there must have been something there?'

'I do.'

The Rector frowned. 'It does rather look as if steps have been taken to conceal certain—er—facts.'

Henrietta tightened her lips. 'It's not going to be easy, is it?'

'What isn't?'

'Finding out who I am.'

*   *   *

Sloan and Crosby saw Constable Hepple soon after they had forked left at the post office. He had brought a plan with him.

'You can't see the chalk lines any more, sir,' he said, 'but deceased was lying roughly here.'

'I see.'

'Walking home and hit from behind, I'd say,' went on Hepple. 'People never will walk towards oncoming traffic like they should.'

'No.'

'His front wheel caught that bit of grass verge afterwards, deflected a bit by the impact, I'd say.'

Sloan nodded.

'I've got a good cast of that,' said Hepple.

Sloan stood in the middle of the bend and looked in both directions. It was a bad bend but with due care and attention there was no need to kill a pedestrian on it.

60

Hepple was still theorising. 'I reckon he didn't see her at all, sir. There's not a suspicion of a skid mark on the road. Daresay he didn't realise what he'd done till afterwards and then he panicked.'

That was the neat and tidy explanation. And, but for Dr Dabbe, it would probably have been the one that went down on the record. Pathology was like that.

'Where exactly did you say she was lying?' asked Inspector Sloan.

Constable Hepple stood squarely on the spot where he had seen the body.

'That,' pronounced Sloan sombrely, 'fits in very well with the first set of injuries . . .'

'The first, sir?' Hepple looked shocked. 'You mean . . .'

'Run over twice,' said Sloan succinctly.

'Once each way,' amplified Crosby for good measure.

'But . . .' Hepple pointed to the patch of road where he was standing. 'But, sir, someone coming the other way—from Belling St Peter—would have had to come onto quite the wrong side of his road to hit her.'

'Yes.'

'But . . .' said Hepple again.

'I am beginning to think someone did come onto quite the wrong side of his road to hit her,' said Sloan, still sombre. 'The pathologist reports that a second car went over her after she was dead.'

'After she was dead?'

'Broke her femur.'

'A second car?' echoed Hepple wonderingly. 'Two cars ran over Mrs Jenkins on this road . . .'

'Yes.'

'. . . and neither of them stopped?' That was the enormity to PC Hepple. A new crime in an irresponsible society, that's what that was, something they'd have been ashamed to put on the Newgate Calendar.

'Two cars,' said Sloan ominously, 'or the first one on its way back.'

Constable Hepple looked really worried. 'I don't like the sound of this at all, sir.'

'No.' Sloan looked at the village constable. 'I don't think I do either.' He examined the road again. 'Now, tell me this—just supposing that it was the same car that hit her both times . . .'

'Yes, sir?' Clearly Hepple didn't like considering anything of the sort.

'Where would he have been able to turn?'

This was where really detailed local knowledge came into its own.

'If he'd wanted to stay on the metalled road, sir, he'd have had to go quite a way. There's no road junction before Belling and this road is too narrow for a really big car to turn in. But if he'd settled for a gateway or the like . . .'

'Yes?'

'Then Shire Oak Farm is the first one you'd

come to beyond the houses. The Thorpes'. After that there's Peterson's and then Smith's ...'

Inspector Sloan sent Crosby off to search for tyre prints. 'It's probably too late, but it's worth a look.' Then he asked Constable Hepple to tell him what he knew about the late Mrs Grace Jenkins of Boundary Cottage.

'Known her for a long time, sir, and always very pleasasnt when we met.' Thinking this might be misconstrued he added hastily, 'Never in the course of duty, mind you, sir. I never had occasion to speak to her in the course of duty. A quiet lady. Kept herself to herself, if you know what I mean.'

Sloan knew and wasn't pleased with the knowledge. Not the easiest sort of person to find out about.

'Tuesday,' he said. 'Did you find out anything about what she'd been doing on Tuesday?'

'She was away from Larking all day,' replied Hepple promptly, 'that's all I know. She went off on the early bus—the one that gets people into Berebury in time for work. And she came back on the last one. Two Larking people got off at the same time. Mrs Perkins and Mrs Callows.'

'Do we—does anyone—know how she spent the day?'

'Not yet, sir. They—Mrs Perkins and Mrs Callows—had been shopping but if Mrs

Jenkins had, I don't know what she'd done with her basket because it wasn't here when I searched yesterday morning.'

'I see.'

'Must have been all of eight o'clock when she was killed,' went on Hepple. 'Allowing for the walk from the post office.'

Sloan stroked his chin. 'Eight o'clock fits in with what the pathologist says.'

'Sir.' The conscientious Hepple was still worried about something.

'Yes?'

'This second accident—was it straight after the first?'

'I don't know. Nobody knows.'

'Oh, I see, sir, thank you.'

'We only know,' said Sloan, 'that she was killed outright by the first one, and that after it another car, or the same car, ran over her.'

Hepple had scarcely finished shaking his head over this before Crosby was back.

'Didn't have to go very far, sir.'

'How far?'

'He—whoever he was—turned in the first farm gateway . . .'

'Shire Oak Farm,' said Hepple. 'The Thorpes'.'

'He was fairly big,' went on Constable Crosby. 'He had to have two goes at it to get round.'

'Yes.' That was what Sloan would have expected.

'The offside rear tyre print's nearly gone—
had some big stuff through that gate since then
I should think.'

'Tractors,' supplied Hepple, 'and the milk
lorry.'

'But there's a good one of a nearside rear.'

Sloan pointed to the grasss verge. 'So we've
got a nearside front tyre print there . . .'

'A good clear one,' contributed Hepple
professionally.

'And a same sized nearside rear-tyre print
turning in the Thorpes' entrance about—how
far away would you say, Crosby?'

'About half a mile.'

Hepple didn't like the sound of that at all.
'So you think he came back this way, sir?'

'I do.'

'He must have seen her the second time,'
persisted Hepple. 'The road isn't wide enough
for him not to have seen her lying across it the
second time even if he didn't the first.'

'I am beginning to think,' said Sloan grimly,
'that he saw her quite well both times.'

'You mean, sir . . .'

'I mean, Hepple, that I think we're dealing
with a case of murder by motor car.'

CHAPTER SIX

The offices of Waind, Arbican and Waind were still in Ox Lane, Calleford.

Inspector Sloan telephoned them from the kiosk outside Larking Post Office. There were, it seemed, no Mr Wainds left in the firm but Mr Arbican was there, and would certainly see Inspector Sloan if he came to Calleford. Sloan looked at his watch and said they might make it by six o'clock. Cross country it must be all of forty miles from Larking to the county town.

They got there at ten minutes to the hour, running in on the road alongside the Minster as most of the population were making their way home. Crosby wove in and out of the crowded streets until he got to Ox Lane.

The solicitors' office was coming to the end of its working day, too. In the outer office a very junior female clerk was making up the post book and two other girls were covering over their typewriters. One of the girls received the policemen and showed them into Mr Arbican's room. The solicitor got to his feet as they entered. He was in his early fifties, going a little bald on top, and every inch the prosperous country solicitor. The room was pleasantly furnished, if a little on the formal side.

'Good afternoon, gentlemen. Do sit down.'

He waved them to two chairs, and said to the girl who had shown them in, 'Don't go yet, Miss Chilvers, will you? I may need you.'

Miss Chilvers looked resigned and returned to the outer office.

Arbican looked expectantly across his desk. It had a red leather top and was in rather sharp contrast to the wooden one at which Sloan worked.

'It's like this, sir,' began Sloan. 'We're in the process of making enquiries about a client of yours . . .'

Arbican raised an eyebrow but said nothing.

'Or it might be more correct,' went on Sloan fairly, 'to say a former client.'

Arbican cleared his throat encouragingly but still did not speak.

'A Mrs Jenkins,' said Sloan.

'Jenkins?' Arbican frowned. 'Jenkins. It's a common enough name but I don't think I know of a client called Jenkins.'

'Jenkins from Larking,' said Sloan.

'Larking?' That's a fair way from here, Inspector. I shouldn't imagine we would have many clients in that direction. You're sure there's no mistake?'

'We are working, sir, on the supposition that she came from East Calleshire before she went to Larking.'

'Ah, yes, I see. Quite possibly. Though I can't say offhand that the name alone means anything to me.' He raised his eyebrows again.

'Should it?'

'We have a letter you wrote . . .'

Arbican's voice was very dry. 'I write a great many letters.'

'To a Mr James Heber Hibbs of The Hall, Larking.'

Arbican shook his head. 'I'm very sorry, Inspector. Neither name conveys anything.'

'That could be so, sir. It was all a long time ago.'

'You're being quite puzzling, Inspector . . .'

'Yes, sir,' said Sloan stolidly. He took out the letter James Hibbs had given him and handed it across the desk to the solicitor. 'Perhaps you'd care to take a look at it.'

Arbican took the letter and read it through quickly. 'I'm sorry I couldn't remember the name but I must have written hundreds of letters like this. In fact, Inspector, it's neither an uncommon name nor an uncommon letter.'

'I suppose not, sir.'

'It was—er—as you say quite a long time ago, too.'

'Over twenty years.'

'Then you can't really have expected me to remember.' He smiled for the first time. A quick professional smile. 'I was a comparative youngster then, cutting my legal teeth on routine where I couldn't do any harm.'

'But you did write it?'

He scanned the letter again. 'I must have done. These are certainly my initials at the top—F. F. A. Therefore,' he frowned, 'therefore we must have done business with this Mrs G. E. Jenkins.' He looked curiously across at Sloan. 'And so?'

'And so you might have some records, sir,' responded Sloan promptly.

'I very much doubt it at this distance of time. We destroy most records after twelve years except conveyances and wills. However, we can soon see.' He rang for Miss Chilvers whose look of patient resignation had changed with the passage of time to one of plain resentment. 'Miss Chilvers, will you please see if we have any records of a Mrs G. E. Jenkins of . . .' (he looked down at the letter) '. . . Boundary Cottage, Larking.'

Miss Chilvers withdrew but her unforthcoming expression started a new train of thought in Sloan's mind. He waved vaguely towards the outer office. 'Perhaps, sir, whoever actually typed the letter might remember. Not Miss Chilvers naturally . . .'

Arbican looked at the letter again and shook his head.

'No?' said Sloan.

'I'm afraid not. I should say that our Miss Lendry typed this letter. Her initials are there after mine—W.B.L.'

'Couldn't she help?'

'No. She isn't with us any more.'

'Perhaps we could find her,' suggested Sloan. 'Do you know her address?'

'I'm sorry. I was using a euphemism.' He sighed. 'Miss Lendry's dead. About six months ago.' He tapped the letter. 'She wouldn't have been all that young when this was written, but she'd have remembered all right.'

'I see.'

'Been with the firm for years,' said Arbican. 'Knew everything . . .'

'Right-hand woman?' suggested Sloan helpfully.

They could hear Miss Chilvers bumping her way round the filing cabinets in the outer office.

Arbican sighed. 'It's not the same without her.'

Sloan knew what he meant. Miss Chilvers returned with little ceremony to announce that she couldn't find anything about a Mrs G. E. Jenkins at all anywhere.

'Thank you,' said Arbican. He turned to Sloan. 'I'm sorry, Inspector, it doesn't look as if we're able to help you with this Mrs Grace Jenkins but if we do come across anything . . .'

Sloan got to his feet. 'Thank you, sir. I'd be much obliged if you'd let me know.'

Arbican handed the letter back. 'Whoever she was, it looks as if she got her settlement all right.'

'Settlement?' said Sloan sharply.

The solicitor pointed to the letter. 'Isn't that what that was?'

'Was it?' countered Sloan.

70

'I can't remember,' said Arbican cautiously, 'but it reads to me now as if it could have been. We advised her to accept the man's offer—that phrasing sounds like a settlement to me but I may be wrong. It's all a long time ago, now, Inspector, and I certainly can't remember.'

*   *   *

'Murder by motor car!' exploded Superintendent Leeyes. 'Are you sure, Sloan?'

'No, sir.' Sloan was both tired and hungry. 'Not yet.'

It was nearly eight o'clock in the evening and they had just got back to Berebury Police Station after an hour's driving along the main road from Calleford.

'But Crosby found some tyre prints in a gateway where the car turned and came back, and Dr Dabbe says she was run over twice.'

'Twice?' said the Superintendent, just as Hepple had done.

'Twice. Once alive, once dead.'

'Macabre chap, Dabbe.'

'Yes, sir.' Sloan paused. 'It's not exactly the sort of road where you could miss seeing someone lying in it.'

'So that makes you think that . . .'

'I think,' said Sloan heavily, 'that she was knocked down from behind on that bend on purpose by someone who afterwards turned in the entrance to Shire Oak Farm and who came

71

back and deliberately hit her again.'

Leeyes grunted.

'Only he had a bit of bad luck.'

'It sounds to me,' said the Superintendent sarcastically, 'as if he wasn't the only one who had a bit of bad luck.'

'No, sir.'

'Well, in what way was he unlucky?'

'He happened to kill her outright the first time he went over her which meant the pathologist knew he'd gone over her twice.'

'How?'

'Because the second lot of injuries were post-mortem ones. They don't bleed,' he added elliptically.

'You wouldn't convince a jury on that alone, Sloan.'

'I shouldn't try,' retorted Sloan spiritedly. 'But it's not alone. Put it together with the breaking into of the bureau and the fact that whoever Grace Jenkins was she wasn't the mother of the girl.'

'Ah, yes. I was forgetting the daughter had been smuggled in in a warming pan.'

'That's about the only explanation that fits at the moment,' agreed Sloan gloomily. 'There's something else, too, sir.'

'What's that?'

'This woman—Grace Jenkins—was having her daughter on about something else. Her age.'

'Her age?'

'Yes, sir. She told the girl she would be forty-six next birthday. Dr Dabbe says she was older than that.'

'He should know, I suppose.'

'Yes, sir.'

'Anything else?'

'She'd had her hair dyed.'

'Who hasn't?' said Leeyes cynically.

'From blonde to brunette.'

'It's usually the other way,' agreed the Superintendent.

'The girl's hair is dark,' said Sloan, 'but the father's is fair—noticeably fair—even in a photograph. Grace Jenkins was fair too—before she had her hair dyed.'

'A pretty puzzle,' Leeyes said unhelpfully.

'Yes, sir. So far we've confirmed that the woman went to Larking when the girl was a small infant and passed her off to everyone as her own.'

'It's been done before.'

'Yes, sir. They rented a small cottage in the grounds of The Hall estate.'

'Buried in the country.'

'Exactly, sir. The rent is very low indeed. Seems almost nominal now but it may have been fair enough at the time. Landlord says he isn't allowed to put it up.'

'He may not have wanted to,' observed Leeyes.

'That thought had occurred to me, sir.'

'That's been done before, too,' said the

Superintendent emphatically.

'What has, sir?'

'Parking an infant in a corner like that. Where you can keep an eye on it.'

'Without acknowledging it?'

'Without acknowledging anything,' Leeyes grunted. 'What's he like?'

'Hibbs? Dark. But it's not a father we're short of, sir, it's a mother.'

'Someone who couldn't acknowledge it either, I daresay,' said the Superintendent.

'Perhaps. Then who is Grace Jenkins?'

'And why kill her?'

'Aunt?' said Sloan as if Leeyes had not spoken. 'Nanny? Or grandmother?'

'Wet nurse, more like,' growled Leeyes.

Sloan told him about the letter and the interview with Arbican. 'He thought the wording read like the outcome of a settlement rather than straightforward renting.'

'There's nothing straightforward about this case,' said the Superintendent irritably. 'Nothing at all.'

'No, sir.'

'We don't even know for a start that the deceased has been correctly identified.'

'We've no evidence either way about that,' said Sloan carefully. 'The only actual evidence we've got that will stand up in a Coroner's Court is that she was childless. We've got none as to who she is.'

'Then,' said the Superintendent brusquely,

74

'you'd better get some, hadn't you, Sloan . . .'

'Yes, sir.'

'. . . and quickly.'

*　　　*　　　*

Henrietta refused to stay the night at the Rectory.

'It's very kind of you,' she said awkwardly. 'Mrs Thorpe asked me to go to Shire Oak as well but I don't think I will all the same. I feel—well—I feel I ought to begin as I mean to go on.'

'You may be right there,' conceded the Rector, though the kind-hearted Mrs Meyton was all protestation. 'I'll just walk back with you, though, and see you safely home.'

'Is it?'

'Is it what?'

'Home,' said Henrietta.

He took the question very seriously. 'You know, what you need is a good solicitor.'

'I feel,' she said fervently, 'as if I need more than that. A magician, at least.'

But she was grateful to him for escorting her home and said so.

He came indoors with her and checked that Boundary Cottage was secure for the night.

Henrietta pointed to the photograph on the mantelpiece. 'Now I know why the police were so interested in my father.'

'Yes.'

75

'I wasn't able to tell them much.'

The Rector nodied slowly. 'Your mother never spoke about him to me.'

'She did to me—but mostly about the sort of person he was. Not,' bitterly, 'concrete facts for policemen.'

'No.'

'And she wasn't my mother.'

'I was forgetting,' he apologised obliquely.

'It's made me realise how little I really know about him too.'

'A sergeant in the East Calleshires,' said Mr Meyton, moving towards the photograph. 'That's definite enough.'

'Yes.'

'And he saw a fair bit of action.'

'Yes.'

'The DCM and the Military Medal, I think,' said the Rector, taking a closer look still. 'Yes, that's right.'

Henrietta opened the bureau drawer. 'They're in here so that's another thing that's definite.'

She pulled open the little drawer inside the bureau and got out the two medal cases. 'Here they are.'

She handed them to the Rector. He flicked them open.

'Henrietta,' he said.

'Yes?'

'These medals . . .'

'Don't tell me,' she said in a voice that was

76

almost harsh, 'that there's something wrong with those too.'

'That chap in the photograph . . .'

'My father.'

'He had the DCM and the Military Medal.'

'I know.'

'These,' the Rector indicated the two in his hand, 'these are the DSO and the MC.'

CHAPTER SEVEN

'Who?' asked Sloan into the telephone.

'A Mr Meyton, sir,' said the Station Sergeant. 'The Rector of Larking.'

'Do you know him, Sergeant?'

'Not to say know him exactly,' replied the sergeant carefully. 'Not him, himself, if you know what I mean. But we know his hat and his gloves and his umbrella—particularly his umbrella. It comes in here practically every time he comes into Berebury. Very clearly marked, though, I will say that for them.'

'Put him through,' said Sloan resignedly.

He listened. Then in a quite different voice, 'Are you sure, sir?'

'Oh, yes, Inspector.' Mr Meyton might forget his hat, gloves and umbrella but not his military history. 'Henrietta showed them to me last night and I took the liberty of taking them home with me for—er—safe keeping.'

'Thank you, sir.'

'And they're quite different. This one was a white enamelled cross pattée with a slightly convexed face. The edge of the cross was gold.'

'And the DCM?'

'Circular and made of silver,' replied the Rector promptly. 'It's connected to a curved scroll clasp, too. The one that was in the bureau has a ring which fits on to a straight clasp.'

'You saw the ribbons on the photograph?' said Sloan, thinking quickly.

'I did indeed. And they're not even similar . . .'

'Oh?'

'The DSO ribbon,' said the Rector, warming to his theme, 'is red with an edging of blue. The DCM one is crimson, dark blue and crimson in equal widths.'

'Yes,' said Sloan thoughtfully, 'there's all the difference in the world, I can see that. What about the other two?'

'The MC and the MM, Inspector? The MC ribbon is white, a sort of purply blue, and white in three equal stripes.' The Rector paused. 'I think I'm right in saying the Military Medal has a narrow white centre stripe with narrow red, then I think it's narrow white, and then two edging stripes of rather wider dark blue on each side.'

'Six—no seven stripes,' said Sloan.

'That's right.'

'Not easily confused even on a photograph.'

'No. It's not the different colours then, of course, it's the widths that you can see.'

'And you can't very well confuse three broad stripes with a ribbon with seven small ones on.'

'No,' agreed the Rector. 'Not easily.'

'I see,' said Sloan slowly.

'The other one was a cross, too,' went on the Rector. 'Whereas the Military Medal is round and attached to a curved scroll clasp.'

'Didn't they have any names on?' asked Sloan. 'I thought they sometimes did.'

'Sometimes,' said the Rector. 'The owner's name, rank and date are usually engraved on the reverse of the MC.'

'Usually?' No one could have called Sloan slow.

'Yes, Inspector. Not on this one. I'm no expert, of course, but I should say . . .'

'Yes, sir?'

'I should say that—er—steps have been taken to remove the owner's name from this one.'

'Would you, sir?' Sloan became extremely alert.

'The back is almost smooth—but not quite.'

'I understand, sir. You've been most helpful. There'll be an explanation, of course, but in the meantime perhaps you would be kind enough to keep them under lock and key until I get to you. I daresay,' he added heavily, 'there will be rhyme to it as well as reason. If you know what I mean, sir.'

'Indeed, yes,' affirmed Mr Meyton. 'There are, of course, matters which are properly mysterious to us in the religious sense but—er—finite matters are always ...'

*   *   *

'No, Inspector,' Henrietta shook her head. 'I can't tell you anything more than that because I don't know anything more.'

'I see, miss. Thank you.' Sloan and Crosby were back in the parlour of Boundary Cottage, sitting where they had been sitting the day before. Then, Henrietta had looked as if she hadn't slept much the previous night.

Now she looked as if she hadn't slept at all.

'The Rector,' she went on wearily, 'just said that they weren't the right medals for the photograph.'

'Yes, miss. He rang me.'

'He took them away.'

'Yes.'

'Inspector ...'

'Yes, miss?'

'Why weren't they taken on Tuesday?'

'On Tuesday, miss?'

'By whoever broke into the bureau.'

'I couldn't say, miss.'

'They must have seen them. They weren't locked up in their cases or anything.'

'No.' He cleared his throat and said

cautiously. 'If they'd gone then, of course, you would have missed them.'

'Naturally.'

'Well, their absence then might have served to call your—call our attention to—er—any irregularities in the situation between you and your—er—parents. If they hadn't been there then we might have started to wonder why not.' Sloan felt himself going a bit hot under the collar. It wasn't a sensation he was accustomed to. 'I don't think it is generally appreciated that the—er—fact of childlessness is—er—established at a routine post-mortem.'

He hadn't appreciated it himself, actually.

Until yesterday.

To his relief Henrietta smiled wanly and said, 'I see.'

'I mean,' expanded Sloan, 'the chances of your discovering that they were the wrong medals . . .'

'Wrong?' she said swiftly.

'Wrong for the photograph.'

'Go on, Inspector.' Warily.

'The chances of them being handled by anyone knowing quite as much about the subject as Mr Meyton were really very slight.'

Since putting down the telephone Sloan had sent Crosby to check up on the Rector's standing as an historian and found it high. Particularly in the field of military history.

'Inspector, are you trying to tell me someone has been unlucky?'

'That's one way of looking at it, miss. But for the accident of the Rector seeing them you might never have known.'

'Known what?' she said with a sigh. 'What exactly does it mean we know now that we didn't know before?'

'That the medals are significant,' said Sloan promptly.

She looked up. 'Do you think so, Inspector?'

'I do, miss, though I don't know what of just yet. Give us a little time.' He hesitated and then said, 'I think we may be going to find the answer to a lot of questions in the past.'

She nodded. 'Twenty-one years ago.'

'Why then?'

'I'll be twenty-one next month. At least I think I will be if my mother . . .'—she corrected herself painfully—'. . . if what I've been told is correct.'

'Twenty-one?' Sloan frowned. 'That could be important.'

'To me, Inspector.' Her voice had an ironic ring. 'The key of the door, perhaps. But not to anyone else.'

'I shouldn't be too sure about that, miss. Not just yet.'

'And it rather looks,' she went on as if she hadn't heard him, 'as if I'm not the only one to have a key to the front door of Boundary Cottage, doesn't it?'

'True.' He paused. 'Yesterday you told me

82

as much as you could remember being told about your father.'

'Yes?'

'What do you know about your . . . about Grace Jenkins?'

It was pitifully little in terms of verifiable fact—if she was telling him the truth. Her mother had been a children's nurse for a family called Hocklington-Garwell, somewhere over the other side of the county. Henrietta didn't know the exact address but she had been brought up on stories of the Hocklington-Garwell children. There had been two of them—both boys. Master Hugo and Master Michael. Then Grace Wright had met Cyril Jenkins, and married him.

'After that,' concluded Henrietta tightly, 'I understood they had had me.'

'I see,' said Sloan.

'And that very soon afterwards my father had been killed.'

'I see,' said Sloan again.

'But they didn't have me,' observed Henrietta astringently.

'*She* didn't,' agreed Sloan. 'The chances of your being your father's child—so to speak— are high.'

'Thank you,' she said gravely. 'I'll remember that.'

'And the chances of her having come from East Calleshire are higher still.' He told her about Messrs Waind, Arbican and Waind in

Calleford. 'So, miss, I think we can take it that the mystery originates that way somewhere.'

He did not mention murder.

*   *   *

'What I want to know,' said the Superintendent testily, 'is not who got which going but what you're doing about it, Sloan.' The Inspector was speaking from the call box in Larking village.

'Yes, sir. In the first instance we are looking for a car which hit a woman . . .'

'An unknown woman,' pointed out Leeyes.

'A woman who may or may not be unknown,' agreed Sloan more moderately, 'which hit her on a bad bend outside Larking village on Tuesday evening sometime between say six and nine o'clock.'

'And have you got anywhere?'

'No, sir.'

'There's an inquest coming along on Saturday morning,' said Leeyes very gently. 'It's the law, Sloan, and the first thing the Coroner does is to take evidence of identification.'

'Yes, sir.' He hesitated. 'We've no reason to suppose she isn't Grace Jenkins . . .'

Superintendent Leeyes gave an intimidating grunt.

'But,' went on Sloan hastily, 'I'm going to make some enquiries about her pension now, and see the two people who came back on the bus with her on Tuesday night. And I've got a man checking up now on the marriage register in Somerset House.'

'What's that going to prove?'

'Whether or not this Grace Edith Wright did, in fact, marry one Cyril Edgar Jenkins. That should give us a lead.'

'One way or the other,' said Leeyes pointedly.

'Exactly, sir. We've got the experts working on those tyre casts too, and we're putting out a general call for witnesses. We're also trying to establish how she spent Tuesday—that may have some bearing on the case . . .'

Leeyes grunted again.

'It's a bit difficult,' said Sloan, 'because the girl has no idea . . .'

'It strikes me that the girl has no idea about too many things.'

'She was away at university at the time.'

'Check up on that, too, Sloan.'

'Yes, sir. This man Hibbs . . .'

'Ah, yes,' ruminatively. 'Hibbs. That solicitor fellow you were talking to yesterday . . .'

'Arbican.'

'He mentioned a settlement, didn't he?'

'Yes, sir.'

'It could have been with Hibbs.'

'Yes, sir. That had already occurred to me.'

'Could he have killed Grace Jenkins?'

'It strikes me,' said Sloan pessimistically,

'that anyone could have killed her. Anyone at all.'

'He's a local,' said Leeyes.

'Yes, sir.'

'He would know about the bend . . .'

'And the last bus.'

'So you see . . .'

'And that it's a deserted road at the best of times, but especially at night.'

'I don't like the country,' declared Leeyes. 'There are never any witnesses.'

'No, sir.'

'Find out what Hibbs was doing on Tuesday night.'

'Yes, sir.'

'What sort of a car has he got?'

'The right sort,' said Sloan cautiously.

'What?'

'That size tyre fits half a dozen cars. He happens to have one of them. A Riley.'

'Was it damaged?'

'I only saw the back.'

'Then take a look at the front, Sloan, somehow. I don't care how.'

Yes, sir.'

*   *   *

'Bill, will you do something for me?'

Bill Thorpe throttled back the tractor to silence point and started to climb down from his high seat. 'Not something.' He grinned.

86

'Anything.'

In spite of all that had happened, Henrietta smiled.

'Changed your mind about coming to the farm to sleep?' asked Bill. 'Mother'll be pleased. She's been worried about you down here on your own these last two nights.'

'No, Bill, it's not that.' Henrietta pulled her coat round her shoulders. 'I'm not leaving Boundary Cottage even for one night.'

'It was just that . . .'

'I feel it's the only link I've got now with things like they used to be.'

'I expect you're bound to feel like that for a bit,' he said awkwardly. 'I daresay it'll wear off after a while.'

'No, it won't . . .'

'I see.'

She shook her head. 'No, you don't, Bill. But—it's difficult to explain—but the cottage and the things in it are the only things that seem real to me somehow.'

'I'm real,' said Bill Thorpe. And indeed he looked it, foursquare against the spring sky.

'I know you are. It's not that.'

'Well, what is it, then?'

She shivered. 'I feel I need to actually see the things I know there. Otherwise . . .'

'Otherwise what?'

'Otherwise,' she said soberly, 'I think I shall go out of my mind.'

'Here,' protested Bill, 'Take it easy. No one

can make you leave if you don't want to.'

'Can't they just!' retorted Henrietta. 'That's what you think, Bill.'

'You're a protected tenant,' insisted Bill firmly. 'No one can make you leave. I'll see to that. Besides, Mr Hibbs would never turn you out. He's not that sort of man.'

'I don't think he would either,' said Henrietta slowly. 'He's always been very kind.' She looked at Bill and opened her eyes wide. 'He's always been very kind.'

'Yes, yes,' said Thorpe impatiently. 'I know. I think you're worrying about nothing.'

'I'm not.' She paused, then, 'Bill . . .'

'Yes?'

'I've got something to tell you.' She swallowed twice in quick succession. 'You're not going to like it.'

'Try me,' he said evenly.

'The police say Grace Jenkins wasn't my mother.' Now it was out she felt better. 'And,' she added defiantly, 'I don't know who was.'

In the event his reaction was surprising.

He kissed her.

And then—

'You don't know how glad I am to hear you say that.'

Henrietta looked up at him in astonishment—he was half a head taller than she was—and said, 'Why?'

'I thought it was me.'

'You thought what was you?'

88

'The reason why your mother wouldn't let us get married.'

'She wasn't my mother,' said Henrietta automatically.

'Exactly.' Bill Thorpe was beaming all over his face.

'I don't see what that's got to do with us not getting married.'

'Don't you?'

'No.'

'Silly.' He looked down at her affectionately. 'We couldn't get married without her permission because you weren't twenty-one.'

'I know that . . .'

'She couldn't give it.'

'Why not?'

'Because she wasn't your mother. You've just said so.'

'I never thought of that,' said Henrietta wonderingly. 'I thought it was only because she wanted me to finish my three years at university.'

'And I thought it was because she didn't like Bill Thorpe,' said Bill Thorpe ruefully.

'And all the time,' whispered Henrietta, 'it was because she didn't want me to know I wasn't hers.'

'Until you were twenty-one,' concluded Thorpe. 'I reckon you were to be told then.'

She shivered. 'Now we may never know.'

'Don't you believe it.'

'Bill . . .' tentatively.

'Yes?'

'There must be some . . . some reason why she didn't want me to know.'

He nodded. 'Knowing your mother I should say a good reason.' He hesitated. 'She'd got all this worked out, hadn't she?'

'It rather looks like it. I . . . I don't know what to think.' Bill Thorpe looked at the sky. It was the subconscious glance of a farmer. 'What was it you wanted me to do, then?'

'Take me to Calleford this afternoon.'

CHAPTER EIGHT

'Where are we now, Crosby?'

It was a rhetorical question. Inspector Sloan and Detective Constable Crosby were, in fact, walking from Boundary Cottage towards Larking Post Office.

'We thought we didn't know about the mother,' responded Crosby. 'Now we don't know about the father either.'

'Not well put, but I am with you.'

'In fact,' went on Crosby morosely, 'we hardly know anything.' He did not like walking.

'We know a woman was killed by a motor vehicle in—er—unusual circumstances.'

They were not far now from the fatal bend in the road. Crosby looked up and down. 'You couldn't not see someone on a road as narrow as this.'

'No.' Sloan reverted to Grace Jenkins. 'We know that she was childless.'

'But,' put in Crosby, 'that she pretended not to be.'

'Just so,' said Sloan. 'An interesting situation.'

'And that's all we do know,' concluded Crosby flatly.

'Try again,' advised Sloan, 'because it isn't.'

Crosby's brow became as furrowed as one of the Thorpes' ploughed fields.

'There's something fishy about the photograph and the medals?'

'There is.' Sloan was already listing in his own mind the enquiries which would have to be made about the photograph and the medals. 'But go back to the woman for a moment . . .'

Crosby's brow resumed its furrows.

'Why,' asked Sloan helpfully, 'was she killed?'

There was a long pause. 'Search me,' said Detective Constable Crosby at long last.

'If Sergeant Gelven wasn't on annual leave, Constable, I wouldn't have to,' said Sloan crisply.

'No, sir.'

They had passed the bad bend now and were walking towards the centre of the village. The Hall lay over on their right, nestled into

91

the folding countryside in the sheltered site chosen in their wisdom by its Tudor builders. It would be in the best situation for several miles around and there would have been a spring or a good well nearby.

They walked past the gates. They were well-hung and newly painted. Nothing, thought Sloan, gave you as good a view of the state of a property as the gates. Mr James Hibbs was clearly a man of means who was prepared to pay attention to detail.

'I think we know why she was killed,' said Sloan.

The church had come into view now. It, too, was on the right of the road. If Sloan knew anything about land-owners there would be a gate through into the churchyard from the grounds of The Hall. The ultimate in status symbols.

'Do we?' said Crosby cautiously.

'You mentioned adoption . . .'

'Yes, sir.'

'There comes a point when—like it or not—it is customary to tell the adopted child the—er—truth about its parents or lack of them.'

'Twenty-one,' said Crosby.

'Just so. All wrong, of course. The right time is before they can understand.'

'Yes, sir. The psychologists say . . .'

'I understand,' said Sloan coldly, not liking the word, 'that you should stress that they are chosen.' He looked Crosby up and down. 'Not an unhappy accident of fate like everyone else's children.'

'No, sir.'

They could see beyond the church now to the Rectory and the patch of grass that presumably did duty as a village green. No one could have called Larking picturesque, although it was by no means unattractive.

'I think she was killed because the girl is going to be twenty-one next month.'

'And someone doesn't want Henrietta to know who she is?' responded Crosby brightly.

'Don't strain yourself thinking too hard, Constable, will you?'

'No, sir.'

'She tells us she is going to be twenty-one in April,' continued Sloan, 'and I think she has been correctly informed on this point, but April would be too late for the killing of Grace Jenkins for two reasons . . .'

He waited hopefully for Crosby to enumerate them.

Crosby said nothing.

'Two reasons,' went on Sloan in a resigned way. When he got back to Berebury he would look up the leave schedules to see when Sergeant Gelven was coming back. They weren't going to solve anything at all at this rate. 'One of them is that the girl would have been back from university by then.'

Crosby nodded in agreement.

'The other is . . .'

'Daylight,' said Crosby unexpectedly.

'Exactly. By April the last bus would be getting to Larking in the twilight rather than the sort of darkness you can easily run someone down in. There's another thing . . .'

Crosby cocked his head like a spaniel.

'This wedding . . .'

'She wouldn't let them get married,' said Crosby. 'That chap Hibbs told us that.'

'Have you thought why not? Thorpe's a nice enough lad by all accounts . . .'

They were right in the centre of the village now and he and Crosby knocked on the door of the house of the last person known to have seen the late Grace Edith Jenkins alive.

'That's right,' said Mrs Martha Callows, not without relish. 'I reckon me and Mrs Perkins was the last to see her. On the last bus, she was, same as we were.'

She admitted the policemen into an untidy house, knocked a cat off one chair, scooped a child out of another and invited them to sit down.

'The last bus from Berebury?' asked Sloan with the air of one anxious to get everything clear.

'There aren't any other buses from anywhere else,' Mrs Callows said, 'and there aren't all that many from Berebury. If you miss the seven-five you walk.'

'Quite so. Was it crowded?'

'Not after Cullingoak. Most people get out

there. Get down, you.' This last was said to the cat, which, thwarted of the chair, was settling on the table.

'Where did you get out?'

'The post office. That's the only stop in Larking. We all got out there. Me and Mrs Perkins and her.'

'About what time would that have been?'

'Something short of eight o'clock.'

The cat had not, in fact, troubled to get down and was now investigating some dirty plates which were still on the table.

'You'd been shopping?' said Sloan generally.

'Sort of. Mrs Perkins—that's who I was with—her husband's in hospital. That's why we was on the late bus. Visiting hours. 'Course, we'd been round the shops first . . . Berebury's a long way to go for nothing.'

'Quite so. Had Mrs Jenkins got a shopping basket?'

'Now I come to think of it,' said Mrs Callows, screwing up her face in recollection, 'I don't know that she had.' Her face cleared suddenly. 'But then she wouldn't have, would she?'

'Why not?' enquired Sloan with interest.

'Friday's her day for Berebury. Not Toosday. She goes in Fridays, regular as clockwork. Always has done.'

'Not Tuesdays?'

Mrs Callows shook her head. 'Not

95

shopping.'

'I see. Tell me,' Sloan was at his most confidential, 'tell me, was she her usual self otherwise?'

A wary look came into Mrs Callows's eye. 'Yes, I suppose you could say she was.'

Sloan tried another tack. 'Cheerful?'

'I wouldn't say cheerful meself. Polite, of course, hoh yes, always very polite was Mrs Jenkins, but not what you'd call cheerful.'

'Talkative sort?'

Mrs Callows shook her head. 'Not ever. Never much to say for herself at the best of times but take Toosday f'r'instance. "Good evening," she says. "We could do with a bit better weather than this, couldn't we? Too windy," And passes right down the bus to the front and sits there by herself.'

'Kept herself to herself?'

'That's right. She did.' Mrs Callows reached out absently and gave the cat a cuff. It retreated, but only momentarily.

'She didn't tell you how she'd spent the day?' asked Sloan.

Mrs Callows sniffed. 'She wouldn't tell us a thing like that. She wasn't the sort.'

'I see.' Sloan reverted to officialese. 'We are naturally anxious to trace Mrs Jenkins's movements on Tuesday . . .'

'There I cannot help,' said Mrs Callows frankly. 'Neither of us set eyes on her until we got to the bus station.'

'What about afterwards?'

'When we got back to Larking, you mean?'

'That's right.' Sloan waved an arm. 'Other people, for instance. Was there anyone about?'

She shook her head. 'We didn't see anybody else, but then we wouldn't, would we?'

'Why not?'

'Because it was Toosday, like I said.'

'Tuesday?'

'The first Toosday,' amplified Mrs Callows. 'Institoot night.'

'I see. So what happened when you all got off the bus?'

'She turned down the lane towards her house. Mrs Perkins and me—we went the other way. That was the last we saw of her.'

'I see,' said Sloan. 'Thank you.'

'It's a nasty bend,' volunteered Mrs Callows suddenly.

'Indeed, yes. By the way, did you see any vehicular traffic?'

Mrs Callows looked blank. 'Oh, you mean cars? No, none at all.'

Sloan and Crosby rose to go.

'Except,' she added, 'the ones parked outside the "King's Head".'

Sloan and Crosby took a look at the 'King's Head' car park on their way from Mrs Callows's house to the post office.

It was an asphalt-affair and disappointing.

'We won't get a tyre print on this.' Crosby stood in the middle of it and stamped his foot.

97

'Hard as iron.'

Inspector Sloan didn't appear to be interested in the surface of the car park. He was moving about and looking down the road to his right.

'Anyway,' went on Crosby, 'she was killed on Tuesday. Today's Friday. Other vehicles would have come in here since then and rubbed them out.'

'What exactly can you see from here, Constable?'

Crosby looked down the road. 'The post office, sir, and a telephone kiosk, the fork in the road to Belling St Peter, the signpost and so forth.' He paused, then, 'A woman pushing a pram, a delivery van, a row of horse-chestnuts . . .'

'This is not a nature ramble, Crosby.'

'No, sir.'

'Anything else?'

'There's the church, sir, beyond the bus stop.'

'Precisely.'

Crosby looked puzzled. 'Is the church important, sir?'

'No.'

'The bus stop?'

'Don't overdo it, Crosby, will you?'

'No, sir.' He turned back to Sloan. 'Where to now, sir?'

'The post office. To see a Mrs Ricks. The admirable Hepple says she knows everything.'

But this was not quite true.

While confirming that the late Grace Jenkins always went into Berebury on Fridays, and seldom, if ever, on Tuesdays, Mrs Ricks was unable to say why she had left on the early bus and come back on the late one. Sloan squeezed alongside a sack of corn while the tall Crosby ducked out of the way of a vicious-looking bill-hook which was suspended from the ceiling. It was above his head—but only just.

'I don't know,' she wheezed regretfully. It was an admission she rarely had to make. 'She wouldn't have said. She wasn't a talker.'

'So I heard,' said Sloan.

'I saw her leave in the morning,' offered Mrs Ricks. 'In her best, she was.'

'Was she?' said Sloan, interested.

'And she was gone all day. At least I never saw her get off a bus before I closed.' Mrs Ricks apparently monitored the bus stop outside the post office window as a matter of course.

'Nasty things, car accidents,' observed Sloan to nobody in particular.

'You needn't think, officer,' said Mrs Ricks, divining his intentions with uncanny accuracy, 'that you'll find anyone to say a word against Mrs Jenkins, because you won't.'

'Madam, I assure you . . .'

'She didn't,' went on Mrs Ricks with the insight born of years of small shopkeeping, 'mix with people enough to upset them, if you see what I mean.'

Sloan saw what she meant.

'Difficult job, all the same,' he said diffidently, 'bringing up a child without a father.'

Mrs Ricks gave a crowing laugh. 'She brought her up all right. She never did anything else all day but look after that child. And that house of hers.'

'Devoted?' suggested Sloan.

Mrs Ricks gave a powerful nod. 'It was always "Henrietta this" and "Henrietta that" with Mrs Jenkins,' she said a trifle spitefully. 'A rare old job it was to get her to take an interest in anything else.'

'I see.'

Mrs Ricks gave a sigh and said sententiously, 'Here today, gone tomorrow. We none of us know, do we, when we shall be called . . .'

Sloan got her back to the point with an effort. 'Do you happen to know which is her pension day?'

'That I do not,' declared Mrs Ricks. 'But I can tell you one thing . . .'

'What's that?'

'That she never got it here.'

'Oh?'

'There's some that don't.' She looked round the crowded little store, saleable goods protruding from every square inch of wall and ceiling space, and lining most of the floor too. 'They like somewhere bigger.'

Sloan saw what she meant. The sales point of the bill-hook was practically making itself felt.

'Especially,' said Mrs Ricks in her infinite wisdom, 'if it isn't as much as they'd like you to think. Sergeant, wasn't he?'

Sloan nodded.

Mrs Ricks sniffed. 'Sometimes they were. Sometimes they weren't.'

*　　　*　　　*

Calleford Minster rose like an *éminence grise* above and behind the clustered shops at the end of Petergate. Mr Arbican of Messrs Waind, Arbican and Waind would be very happy to see Henrietta but her appointment with him was not until a quarter to three. Farmers as a race lunch early and Henrietta and Bill Thorpe had time to spare.

Henrietta turned towards the Minster. 'It's lovely, isn't it?'

Bill Thorpe turned an eye on the towering stone. 'It's more than lovely. Do you realise it could be useful to you?'

'To me?'

He nodded. 'That chap in the photograph . . .'

'My father,' responded Henrietta a little distantly.

'He was—what did you say?—a sergeant in

the East Calleshires?'

'That's right. What about it?'

'He was killed, wasn't he?'

She flushed. 'So I understand.'

'Well, then . . .'

'Well then what?'

'Calleford's their town, isn't it?'

Henrietta sighed. 'Whose town?'

'The East Calleshires,' explained Bill Thorpe patiently. 'The regiment. They've got their barracks here. Like the West Calleshires have theirs in Berebury.'

'What if they have?'

He pointed to the Minster. 'If this is their home town then I think we might find their memorial in the Minster here, don't you?'

'I hadn't thought of that,' she said slowly. 'He—my father—'ll be there, won't he?'

Bill Thorpe led the way towards the Minster gate. 'We can soon see.'

The East Calleshires did have their memorial in the Minster. Henrietta followed Bill Thorpe into the Minster and down the nave. She lagged behind slightly as if she did not want to be there, glancing occasionally at the memorials to eighteenth-century noblemen and nineteenth-century soldiers.

An elderly verger led them to the East Calleshire memorial on the north wall of the north transept.

'It catches the afternoon light just here, you know,' he said. 'Nice piece of marble, isn't it?'

'Very,' said Bill Thorpe politely.

'They couldn't get no more like it,' the man said. 'Not when they came to try. Still, they weren't to know they were going to need a whole lot more less than thirty years later, were they?'

Bill Thorpe nodded in agreement. 'Indeed not. That knowledge was spared them.'

'So that,' went on the man, 'come 1945 they decided they would put those new names on these pillars that were there already. Quite a saving, really, though the money didn't matter, as it happened.' He sighed. 'Funny how often it works out like that, isn't it?'

'Very,' said Bill Thorpe.

'The same crest did, too.' It was obvious that the man spent his days showing people round the Minster. His voice had a sort of hushed monotone suitable to the surroundings. 'That's a nice bit of work, though they tell me it's tricky to dust. They don't think of that sort of thing when they design a monument.'

'I suppose not.'

The verger hitched his gown over his shoulders. 'You two come to look somebody up?'

'Yes,' said Bill. 'Yes, we have.'

'Thought so. People never ask unless they particularly want to see someone they was related to.' He looked them up and down and said tersely, 'First lot or second?'

'Second.'

He sucked his breath in through gaps in his teeth. 'It'll be easier to find then.'

' "An epitaph on an army of mercenaries",' said Bill Thorpe sadly as the old man wandered off.

Henrietta wasn't listening.

'Bill.' She tugged his sleeve urgently. 'Look.'

'Where?'

She pointed. 'There . . .'

'It goes,' agreed Bill Thorpe slowly, 'from Inkpen, T. H. to Jennings, C. R.'

'There's no one called Jenkins there at all,' whispered Henrietta.

CHAPTER NINE

Bill Thorpe shifted his weight from one foot to the other and considered the matter.

'He should have been here, shouldn't he?'

'He was in the East Calleshires,' insisted Henrietta. 'My mother always said he . . . I was told he was but there's the photograph too.'

'The man in the photograph was wearing their uniform.'

'Exactly,' said Henrietta.

'But that's all.'

'All?'

'All you know for sure,' said Thorpe flatly.

Henrietta turned a bewildered face back to

104

the memorial. 'Do you mean the man in the photograph wasn't killed?'

Bill ran his eye down the names. 'He may have been killed and not called Jenkins.'

'Or,' retorted Henrietta astringently, 'I suppose he may have been called Jenkins and not been killed.'

'That is the most probable explanation,' agreed Thorpe calmly.

'How—how am I going to find out?'

'Did you ever see your mother's pension book?'

'She didn't cash her pension at the post office,' she said quickly. 'She took it to the bank. She told me that. Then she used to cash a cheque.'

'I see.'

There was a long pause and then Henrietta said, 'So that, whether or not he was my father, he wasn't killed in the war, was he?'

'Not if he was in the East Calleshires and was also called Jenkins,' agreed Bill Thorpe, pointing to the memorial. 'Of course there is another possibility.'

Henrietta sighed but said nothing.

'He might not have been killed on active service,' went on Thorpe.

'You mean he might have died a natural death?'

'People do, you know,' said Thorpe mildly. 'Even in wartime.'

She was silent for a moment. Then,

'Nothing seems to make sense any more.'

'Everything has an explanation.'

'This must sound very silly,' she said, choosing her words carefully, 'but let me say what I know for certain. There is a photograph . . .'

'The photograph is a fact,' acknowledged Bill Thorpe.

'Which you have seen.'

'Then the photograph is doubly a fact,' he murmured ironically.

'There is a photograph of a man in the uniform of this regiment in the drawing-room at home, and . . .'

'And that,' said Bill Thorpe, 'is all you know for certain.'

She stared at him. 'A man who I thought was my father.'

'Ah, that's different.'

'Who I thought was called Jenkins.'

'Who may or may not be called Jenkins.'

'And who I thought was killed in the war.'

Bill Thorpe pointed to the memorial again. 'Don't you see that he might be called Jenkins or he might have been killed in the war—but not both. The facts are mutually exclusive—unless he changed regiments halfway through or something out of the ordinary like that.'

'Or died a natural death,' persisted the girl.

'Or a very unnatural one,' retorted Thorpe.

Henrietta waited.

'Well,' said Thorpe defensively, 'if he'd been

106

shot as a spy or a deserter or something like that . . .'

'I hadn't thought of that.'

'. . . we're hardly likely to find his name here, are we?' Bill waved a hand which took in all the hallowed thirteenth-century stone about them.

'That means,' decided Henrietta logically, 'that you don't think the man in the photograph is . . . or was my father.'

'There is something wrong about the medals . . .'

'There's something wrong about everything so far,' rejoined Henrietta. 'We're collecting quite a bit of negative evidence.'

'Just as useful as the other sort,' declared Thorpe.

'I'm glad to hear it,' she said rather tartly. 'At the moment the only thing we seem to be absolutely sure about is that there is a photograph of a sergeant in the East Calleshires which has been standing in Boundary Cottage ever since I can remember.'

'The photograph is a fact,' agreed Bill Thorpe with undiminished amiability.

'And so is the name of Jenkins not being on this memorial.'

'The evidence is before our very eyes, as the conjurors say.'

'And the police say Grace Jenkins wasn't my mother.'

Bill Thorpe looked down at her

affectionately. 'I reckon that makes you utterly orphaned, don't you?'

She nodded.

'Quite a good thing, really,' said Thorpe easily.

Henrietta's head came up with a jerk. 'Why?'

'I don't have to ask anyone's permission to marry you.'

She didn't respond. 'I'm worse than just orphaned. I don't even know who I am or who my parents were.'

'Does it matter?'

'Matter?' Henrietta opened her eyes very wide.

'Well, I can see it's important with—say—Shire Oak Majestic. A bull's got to have a good pedigree to be worth anything.'

'I fail to see any connection,' said Henrietta icily.

'I'm not in love with your ancestors . . .'

The verger ambled up behind them. 'Found what you were looking for, sir, on that memorial?'

'What's that? Oh, yes, thank you, verger,' said Thorpe. 'We found what we were looking for all right.'

'That's good, sir. Good afternoon to you both.'

*   *   *

Not unexpectedly, Mr Felix Arbican of Messrs Waind, Arbican and Waind, Solicitors, shared Henrietta's view rather than Bill Thorpe's on the importance of parentage. He heard her story out and then said, 'Tricky.'

'Yes,' agreed Henrietta politely. She regarded that as a gross understatement.

'It raises several—er—legal points.'

'Not only legal ones,' said Henrietta.

'What's that? Oh, yes, quite so. The accident, for instance.' Arbican made a gesture of sympathy. 'I'm sorry. There are so many cars on the road these days.' He brought his hands up to form a pyramid under his chin. 'She was walking, you say . . .'

'She was.'

'Then there should be less question of liability.'

'There is no question of where the blame for the accident lies,' said Henrietta slowly. 'Only the driver still has to be found.'

'He didn't stop?'

She shook her head.

'Nor report it to the police?'

'Not that I've heard.'

'That's a great pity. If he had done, there would have been little more to do—little more from a professional point of view, that is, than to settle the question of responsibility with the insurance company and agree damages.'

Henrietta inclined her head in silence.

'And they usually settle out of court.'

Henrietta moistened her lips. 'There is to be an inquest . . . on Saturday morning.'

'Naturally.'

'Is Berebury too far for you to come?'

'You want me to represent you? If your—er—mother was a client of mine at one time—and it seems very much as if she must have been, then I will certainly do that.'

'The Inspector told me she came to you once . . .'

'A long time ago.'

'You don't recall her?'

Arbican shook his head.

Henrietta lapsed back in her chair in disappointment. 'I was so hoping you would. I need someone who knew her before very badly . . .'

'Quite so.' The solicitor coughed. 'I think in these—er—somewhat unusual circumstances my advice would be that you should first establish if a legal adoption has taken place. That would put a different complexion on the whole affair. You say there are no papers in the house whatsoever?'

'None. There was this burglary, you see . . .'

Arbican nodded. 'It doesn't make matters easier.'

'No.'

'In the absence of any written evidence we could begin a search of the court adoption registers . . .'

Henrietta looked up eagerly.

'But it will necessarily be a slow business. There are about forty County Courts, you see, and—er—several hundred Magistrates' Courts.'

'I see.'

'A will,' said Arbican cautiously, 'might clarify matters.'

'In what way?'

'It would perhaps refer to the relationship between you and Grace Jenkins. Whilst not being her—er—child of the body you could still stand in a legal relationship to her.'

'I don't see how.'

'Have you thought that you could be a child of an earlier marriage of one of the two parties?'

She sighed. 'I don't know what to think.'

'If that were so then you must have been the child of one of them . . .'

'Not Grace Jenkins,' said Henrietta.

'If you aren't,' went on the solicitor, 'and the fact of this in each case can be proved, then you could be a child of a marriage, the surviving partner of which subsequently married one of the two persons whom you have hitherto considered your parents . . .'

She put her hands up to her head. 'You're going too quickly.'

'That would entail a third marriage on someone's part—but three marriages are not out of place these days.'

'It—it's very complicated, isn't it?'

'The law,' said Arbican cheerfully, 'is.'

She hesitated. 'Mr Arbican, if I were illegitimate?'

The solicitor's fingers came up under his chin again while he pontificated. 'The law is much kinder than it used to be, and if your— the person whom you thought to be your mother has made a will in your favour it is of little consequence.'

'It isn't that,' said Henrietta quickly. 'Besides we—she had no money. I know that.'

Arbican looked as if he was about to say that that was of no consequence either.

'In any case,' went on Henrietta, 'I wouldn't want to claim anything I wasn't entitled to, and if she wasn't my mother, I don't see how I can be.'

'A will,' began Arbican, 'would . . .'

'She may not have made one,' countered Henrietta. 'She wasn't expecting to die.'

'Everyone should make a will,' said the solicitor sententiously.

*　　　*　　　*

While farmers lunch early, and clergy at exactly one-fifteen, policemen on duty lunch not at all. Inspector Sloan and Constable Crosby found themselves back in the Berebury Police Station after two-thirty with the canteen offering nothing more substantial than tea and sandwiches. Crosby laid the tray on Sloan's desk.

'It's all they had left,' he said briefly.

'Somerset House didn't have anything either,' Sloan told him, pushing a message pad across the desk. 'No record of any Grace Edith Wright marrying any Cyril Edgar Jenkins within five years of either side of when the girl thought they did.'

Crosby took another sandwich and thought about this for the length of it. Then, 'Grace Jenkins must have had a birth certificate.'

'Wright,' said Sloan automatically.

Crosby, who thought Sloan had said 'Right,' looked pleased and took another sandwich.

'Though,' continued Sloan, 'if she's Wright, why bring Jenkins in at all, especially if she's not married to him.'

Crosby offered no opinion on this.

'Moreover, where do you begin to look?'

'Where, sir?' he echoed.

'Where in time,' explained Sloan kindly. 'Not where in space. It'll all be in Somerset House. It's a question of knowing where to look. The girl tells us Grace Jenkins was forty-five years. The pathologist says she was fifty-five or thereabouts.'

'Yes,' agreed Crosby helpfully.

'And that's not the only thing. The girl says she was married to one Jenkins, deceased, and her maiden name was Wright. Somerset House can't trace the marriage and Dr Dabbe thinks she was both unmarried and childless.'

'More tea?' suggested Crosby constructively.

'Thank you.' Sloan reached for his notebook. 'We can't very well expect the General Register Office to give us the birth certificate of someone whose age we don't know and whose name we aren't sure about. So, instead . . .'

'Yes, sir?'

'You will start looking for a family called—what was it?—ah, yes: a family called Hocklington-Garwell. And a farm.'

'A farm sir?'

'A Holly Tree Farm, Crosby.'

'Somewhere in England, sir?'

'Somewhere in Calleshire,' snapped Sloan.

Crosby swallowed. 'Yes, sir.'

Sloan read through the notes of the interview with Mrs Callows. 'Then there's the bus station. Grace Jenkins arrived there on Tuesday morning and left there on the seven-five in the evening. See if you can find any lead on where she went in between.'

'Yes, sir.'

'Do you remember what it was that was unusual about her on Tuesday?'

'She was killed?'

'Try again, Constable . . .' dangerously.

Crosby frowned. 'She was dressed in her best . . .'

'Anything else?'

'It wasn't her day for shopping in Berebury.'

'Exactly.'

'You could just say it wasn't her day,' murmured Crosby, but fortunately Inspector Sloan didn't hear him.

* * *

Henrietta came out of the offices of Waind, Arbican and Waind, and stood on the pavement. Bill Thorpe was a little way down the road and she waved. He turned and came towards her asking, 'Any luck?'

'None,' Henrietta said despondently. 'He doesn't remember her at all.'

'What about the legal side?' He fell in step beside her. 'I've found a tea-shop down this lane.'

'The legal side!' echoed Henrietta indignantly. 'I'd no idea adoption was so easy. And there's no central register of adoption either.' There was quite a catch in her voice as she said, 'I could be anybody.'

'We'll have to get the vet to you after all. Turn left at this corner.'

Her face lightened momentarily. 'Strangles or spavin?'

'To look at your back teeth,' said Bill Thorpe. He pushed open the door of the tea-shop. They were early and the place was not full. He chose the table at the window and they settled into chairs facing each other.

Henrietta was not to be diverted. 'I am a

person . . .'

'Undoubtedly. If I may say so, quite one of the . . .'

'You may not,' she said repressively.

'Tea, I think, for two,' he said to the waitress. 'And toast.'

'When I was a little girl,' said Henrietta, 'I used to ask myself, "Why am I me?" Now I'm grown up I seem to be asking myself "Who am I?"'

'Philosophy is so egocentric,' complained Bill Thorpe, 'and everyone thinks it isn't. I'm not at all sure I like the idea of your studying it.'

'I'm me,' declared Henrietta.

'And very nice, too, especially your . . .'

'I know I'm me, but where do we go from here?'

Bill Thorpe stirred. 'Your existence isn't in doubt, you know. Only your identity.'

'Then who on earth am I?'

'I don't know,' he said placidly, 'and I don't really care.'

Henrietta did. 'At this rate I could be anybody at all.'

'Not just anybody.'

'There are over fifty million people in this country and if I'm not called . . .'

'We can narrow the field a bit.'

'You're sure?'

'Unless I'm very much mistaken,' he underlined the words, 'you're female. That

116

brings it down to twenty-five million for a start.'

'Bill, be serious. This is important.'

'Not to me, it isn't. But if you insist . . .'

'I do.'

'Then you're a leucodermii.' He grinned. 'That's silenced you. I did anthropology for a year. Enjoyed it, too.'

She smiled for the first time that day. It altered her appearance beyond measure. 'Science succeeding where philosophy has failed, Bill?'

'Well, you're the one who wants to find out who you are. Not me.'

She lowered her eyes meekly. 'And you tell me I'm a leucodermii.'

He waved a hand. 'So you are. If I said "Come hither, my dusky maiden", you needn't come.'

That startled her. 'I'm English.'

It was his turn for irony. 'White, through and through?'

She flushed. 'Not that, but surely . . . I never thought I could be anything but English. Oh, I am. Bill, I must be.'

'Indo-European anyway.' He moved his chair back while the waitress set the tea in front of them. 'Thank you.' While Henrietta poured out, he squinted speculatively at her. 'Your head's all right.'

'Thank you.'

'Mesocephalic. Not long, not broad, but

117

medium.'

'That sounds English if anything does.'

'The lady mocks me.' He held up a hand and ticked off the fingers one by one. 'You're not Slav, nor Mongol . . .'

'Thank you.'

'. . . nor Mediterranean type. If your cheekbones had been a fraction higher, you could have been Scandinavian . . .'

'I feel English.'

'Nurture not nature.'

'I hadn't thought of that.'

'Unless you believe in all this inherited race consciousness theory.'

She shook her head. 'I don't know enough about it.'

'Nobody does. Have some toast. Then I think all we can conclude is that you are free, white and nearly twenty-one.'

'Free?' echoed Henrietta.

'Remarkably so. No attachments whatsoever. Except to me, of course.'

She wouldn't be drawn but sat with her head turned away towards the window, staring at the street.

' "Free as nature first made man",' quoted Bill.

'You'll be talking of noble savages in a minute, I suppose.'

'Never!'

'Tell me this,' she said. 'Do vets still go in for branding?'

'Sometimes,' he said cautiously. 'Why?'

'Because a few marks on my ear at birth would have saved a lot of trouble all round, that's why.'

'You'd better have another cup of tea,' he said. 'And some more toast.'

She refilled her cup and his, and sat gazing through the teashop window at the passers-by.

Suddenly she let her cup fall back into her saucer with an uncontrolled clatter. 'Bill, look. Out there.'

'Where?'

'That man.' She started to struggle to her feet, her face quite white.

'What about him?'

She was pointing agitatedly towards the back of a man walking down the street. 'It . . . it's the man in the photograph . . . Oh, quickly. I'm sure it is.'

'You mean your father?' He pushed his chair back.

'Cyril Jenkins,' she said urgently. 'I swear it is. It was exactly like the man in the photograph, but older.' She started to push her way out of the tea-shop. 'Come on, Bill, quickly. We must catch him whatever happens.'

CHAPTER TEN

It was well after four o'clock before Inspector Sloan and Constable Crosby met again. Crosby went into Sloan's room at the Berebury Police Station waving a list.

'Nearly as long as my arm, sir, this.'

'It can't be as long as your face, Crosby. What is it?'

'The Holly Tree Farms in Calleshire.'

'Routine is the foundation of all police work, Constable. You should know that.'

'Yes, sir. Records have come through on the 'phone, too, sir. They've got nothing against any Cyril Edgar Jenkins or Grace Edith Wright.'

'Or Jenkins.'

'Or Jenkins.'

'That doesn't get us very far then.'

'No, sir.' Crosby still sounded gloomy. 'And I can't get anywhere either with this family that the girl says her mother used to work for.'

'Hocklington-Garwell?' Inspector Sloan frowned. 'I was afraid of that. They may not have lived in Calleshire, of course . . .'

'No, sir. I'd thought of that.' Crosby looked as if he might have to take on the world.

'And there is always the possibility that the girl may be having us on.'

'You mean they might not exist?' If Crosby's

120

expression was anything to go by, this was not quite cricket.

'I do.'

Crosby looked gloomier still. 'It's a funny name to be having us on with, sir, if you know what I mean.'

'That, Constable, is the most sensible remark you've made for a long time.'

'Thank you, sir.'

'Therefore I am inclined to think that the Hocklington-Garwells do exist.'

'Not in Calleshire, sir,' said Crosby firmly. 'Several Garwells but no Hocklingtons and not a sniff of a Hocklington-Garwell.'

'Give me the Garwells's addresses then,' said Sloan. 'We've got to start somewhere and we're getting nowhere fast at the moment.'

'It would have been a lot simpler,' said Crosby plaintively, 'if she had had the baby and we were looking for the father.'

*   *   *

Superintendent Leeyes said much the same thing in different words a few minutes later in his office in the same corridor.

'I've dealt with a few paternity orders in my time, Sloan, but I'm damned if I've met a maternity one yet.'

'No, sir.' He coughed. 'This case has several unusual features.'

'You can say that again,' said his superior

121

encouragingly. 'Found out whose the medals were?'

'Not yet, sir. The old boy at the Rectory's quite right. Knows his stuff. They're the wrong ones for the photograph quite apart from the fact that the DSO and MC are never awarded to sergeants.'

'Officers, medals, for the use of.'

'Yes, sir.'

'This man Hibbs at The Hall. He an officer type?'

'Yes, sir.'

'Hrrrmph.'

'I've had a look at his car,' said Sloan hastily. 'It looks all right to me. It's not all that new and I don't know how much damage to expect to the car from her injuries. I'll have a word with Traffic about that. And Dr Dabbe.'

'And check,' growled Leeyes, 'that he hasn't had them repaired. Plenty of time for that since Tuesday.'

'Yes, sir.'

'What was he doing on Tuesday evening anyway?'

'Nothing,' said Sloan cautiously.

'Nothing?'

'He was alone at home.'

'Was he indeed? Interesting.'

'You see, sir, it was the first Tuesday in the month.'

'I am aware of that, Sloan, but the significance eludes me . . .'

'That's Institoot—I mean, Institute night.'

'You don't say.'

'Mrs Hibbs,' said Sloan hurriedly, 'is Branch President. So she was out.'

'No servants?'

'A daily. A real one.'

'A real one?'

'Comes every day. Daily.'

'There's no need to spell it out for me, man.'

'No, sir.'

'What you are trying to tell me—and taking the devil of a long time about it, if I may say so—is that James Heber Hibbs was alone all evening at The Hall, he has a car whose tyre marks correspond with those found at the scene of the accident and you aren't yet sure if he killed Grace Whatever-her-name is.'

'Yes, sir.'

'Anything else?'

'There may well be something odd about this chap Jenkins, sir, apart from the medals.'

'You can say that again,' responded Leeyes generously. 'I've been making a few enquiries about his pension.'

'Oh?'

'And I can't trace it. It wasn't paid out via the local village post office which is not all that surprising, but it didn't go into her bank account either. I've just seen the manager. No pension voucher record there. Her account was kept going with a small regular monthly cash payment over the counter.'

'Who by?' sharply.

'Grace Jenkins herself to all intents and purposes,' sighed Sloan. 'According to the paying-in slips, she always handed it over herself.'

'Maintenance,' concluded Leeyes.

'Yes, sir, with any clue to its source carefully concealed.'

'And anything not concealed equally carefully removed from the bureau on Tuesday.'

'Just so,' agreed Sloan.

'From what you've said so far,' said the Superintendent, 'she doesn't strike one as having been a kept woman.'

'Only literally, sir, if you follow me. I think it was the child who was kept. I've got in touch with the pension authorities and they're doing a bit of checking up now but it'll take time. It's not as if it were an uncommon name even.'

'No.' The Superintendent thought for a moment and then said, 'The most interesting question from our point of view is: who was keeping both of them?'

'Yes, sir.'

'And why.' The Superintendent sat silent, thinking. Sloan knew better than to interrupt his thoughts. 'If,' said Leeyes at last, 'we knew why they were being kept I daresay we'd know who killed the woman.'

'Whatever the story,' said Sloan, 'I think we

can be fairly sure the situation changed when the girl reached twenty-one.'

'And someone didn't like it the new way.'

'No.'

'That means there's money somewhere, Sloan, or I'm a Dutchman.'

'Perhaps.' Sloan tapped his notebook. 'It could be a question of inheritance easily . . .'

'Or concealment of birth.'

'I'd thought of that, sir. I've been on to the General Register Office with the only reasonable thing I could think of to ask them.'

'What was that?'

'A list of the female children born about the same time as Henrietta Jenkins says she was and who have the same Christian names.'

'That's a tall order,' said the Superintendent.

'They said it would take time,' agreed Sloan dubiously. 'I don't suppose a Friday afternoon's the best moment to ask them either.'

'No.' Leeyes looked at his watch. 'Late on Friday afternoon at that.'

'She was called Henrietta Eleanor Leslie though.'

'That's better than Mary, I suppose.'

'But you don't have to register a birth for six weeks and . . .'

'And,' said the Superintendent grimly, 'we've only got her word for it that those are her names and that that is when she was born.'

'Just so,' said Sloan.

That was the moment when the telephone began to ring.

Leeyes picked it up, listened for a moment and then handed it over to Sloan. 'A call for Inspector Sloan from Calleford. Urgent and personal.'

Sloan took the receiver in one hand and a pencil in the other. 'Speaking . . .'

He listened attentively, then he asked two questions in quick succession, advised the speaker to go home, and replaced the receiver.

'That was Bill Thorpe, sir.'

Leeyes nodded. 'That's the chap who helped find the body, isn't it? The one the girl wanted to marry . . .'

'Him,' said Sloan. 'He's with the girl in Calleford now and she's just seen Cyril Jenkins.'

'Who?' roared Leeyes.

'Cyril Jenkins.'

'He's dead.'

'Not if she's just seen him,' said Sloan reasonably.

'How does she know it's him?'

'Living image of the man in the photograph but older.'

'She's imagining it then.'

'She swears not.'

'Wishful thinking.'

'A dead likeness,' said Sloan pithily. 'That's what Thorpe said.'

126

'Did he see him himself?'

'No. Not his face. Just his back.'

'I don't like it, Sloan.'

'No, sir.' He waited. 'There's something else.'

Leeyes's head came up with a jerk. 'What?'

'They've been in the Minster looking at the East Calleshire's Memorial there.'

'Well?'

'Jenkins's name isn't on it, and he was supposed to have been killed in the war.'

'Well, if he's alive and kicking in Calleford this afternoon that's hardly surprising, is it? Be logical, Sloan.'

'Yes, sir.' You couldn't win. Not with Superintendent Leeyes.

'And I suppose they let him get away.'

'They were in a tea-shop, sir. By the time they got out he'd disappeared.'

'So we don't know if the girl was right or wrong?'

'Strictly speaking, no.'

'And we don't know either, Sloan, if she is having us all on, the Thorpe boy included.'

'No, sir.'

'If she is, do you realise that nearly all the evidence we've got—if you can call it evidence—comes from her?'

'Yes, sir. Apart from Dr Dabbe, that is . . .'

'It's a lonely furrow,' agreed Leeyes sardonically, 'that the doctor's ploughing. What did you tell them to do?'

'Go home to Larking,' said Sloan. 'As the crow flies they're nearer there than they are to Berebury. I'll go down to Larking to see them later.'

Leeyes grunted.

'And,' continued Sloan, 'I'll get some copies of Jenkins's photograph blown up and rushed over to Calleford. No harm in looking for him . . .'

'No harm in finding him,' retorted Leeyes meaningfully. 'It'll be interesting to see if they can pick him up over there. I understand that they can do almost anything at Headquarters.'

'Yes, sir.' The Superintendent pursued his own private vendetta with County Constabulary Headquarters at Calleford.

'Of course,' blandly, 'he may not be called Jenkins.'

'No,' agreed Sloan dutifully.

'And that won't make it any easier for them.'

He did not sound particularly sorry about this.

*　　*　　*

Sloan went into Traffic Division on his way back from seeing the Superintendent. A lugubrious man called Harpe was in charge. He had a reputation for having never been known to smile, which reputation he hotly defended on the grounds that there had never been anything to smile about in Traffic

128

Division. He was accordingly known as Happy Harry.

So it was now.

'Nothing's turned up, Sloan,' he said unsmilingly. 'Not a thing. No witnesses. No damaged cars. Nobody reported knocking a woman down.'

'Where do you usually go from here?'

'Inquest. Newspaper publicity. Radio appeal for eyewitnesses to come forward.'

'Any response as a rule?'

'It all depends,' said Harpe cautiously. 'Usually someone comes forward. Not always.'

'They won't this time,' prophesied Sloan. Harpe's pessimism was infectious.

'Don't suppose they will. Lonely road. Unclassified, isn't it? Nobody about. Dark. Pubs open. Shops shut.'

'Institute night.'

'What's that?'

'Nothing.'

'Our chaps have been in all the local repair garages—no one's brought in anything suspicious, but then if they were bent on not coming forward they'd go as far afield as they conveniently could.'

'Or not repair at all.'

Harpe looked up. 'How do you mean?'

'If this was murder,' said Sloan, 'they'd be dead keen on not getting caught.'

'I'll say.'

'Well, I don't think they'd risk having tell-tale repairs done in Calleshire.'

'They might sell,' said Harpe doubtfully. 'We could get County Hall to tell us about ownership changes if you like.'

'I wasn't thinking of that, though it's a thought. No, if I'd done a murder with a motor car and got some damage to the front . . . how much damage would it be, by the way?'

Harpe shifted in his chair. 'Difficult to say. Varies a lot. Almost none sometimes. Another time it can chew up the front quite a lot. Especially if the windscreen goes.'

'It didn't,' said Sloan. 'There was no glass on the road at all. We looked.'

'That means his headlamps were all right then, too, doesn't it?'

Sloan nodded.

'Of course,' went on Harpe, with the expert's cold-blooded logic, 'if you're engineering your pedestrian stroke vehicle type of accident on purpose . . .'

'I think we were.'

Harpe shrugged. 'If you can afford to wait until you can see the whites of their eyes, then naturally you pick your spot.'

'How do you mean?'

'You hit them full on.'

'Amidships, so to speak?'

'Between the headlamps,' said Harpe seriously. 'You wouldn't break any glass then.'

'I see,' said Sloan.

'Of course, your "exchange principle" still

applies.'

'What's that?'

'Car traces on the pedestrian. Pedestrian traces on the car. Paint, mostly, in the first case . . .'

'Dr Dabbe didn't say and he never misses anything.'

'Blood stains on the car,' went on Harpe cheerlessly, 'and hair and fibres of clothing—only you haven't got the car, have you?'

'No,' said Sloan. 'Then, to go back to concealing the damage . . .'

'If you didn't want to take it anywhere to repair . . .'

'I know what I'd do.'

Harpe looked at him uncomprisingly. 'Well, and what would you do?'

'Bash it into a brick wall,' said Sloan cheerfully. 'Or arrange another accident that would destroy all traces of the first. That would make him safe enough if they did find the car.'

Even then Harpe did not smile.

*   *   *

It was about a quarter to six when Henrietta and Bill Thorpe got back to Boundary Cottage, Larking.

Henrietta went straight through into the front room and halted in her tracks. Bill nearly bumped into her.

'Oh, I'd forgotten,' she said.

'What?'

'The Police Inspector took the photograph away with him.'

'Why?'

'The medals,' said Henrietta vaguely. 'He was going to talk to the Rector about them.'

'There's a fair bit of talking needing doing,' said Bill, settling himself in a chair. 'Am I glad you're going to be twenty-one next month!'

'Why?' She hardly bothered to turn her head.

'Because if we've got to find this character Jenkins and ask his permission for you to marry me we're in real trouble.'

'He's not my father,' said Henrietta. 'My father's dead.'

'How do you know?'

'I don't,' she agreed miserably. 'I don't know anything. I don't even know what I know and what I don't know.'

Bill Thorpe nodded comprehendingly. 'I follow you—though thousands wouldn't. All the same, I'm glad that we'll be able to get to the altar without him. Shouldn't know where to begin to look.'

'It was him,' she said in the tone of one who has said the same thing many times before. 'I'd know him anywhere again. I knew that photograph like the back of my hand.'

'So you said before.'

'He was older, that's all.'

'Twenty years older?'

'About.' She sat down too. 'Men don't change all that much.'

'Sorry to hear you say that.' Bill Thorpe grinned and ran a hand over his face. 'There's room for improvement here. Or do you like me as I am?'

She made a gesture with her hand. 'I can't like you, Bill—I can't like anyone at the moment. Not until I know who I am. Oh, I can't put it into words but there just isn't any of me left over for things like that. Besides, you must know who it is you're marrying.'

'You,' said Bill Thorpe promptly. 'And very nice, too.'

'Bill, do be serious.'

'I am,' he said. 'Deadly. I want to marry you. You as you are now.'

She shook her head. 'I'm too confused. I don't know what I want.'

'I do,' he said simply. 'You.'

She turned away without speaking.

Bill Thorpe was not disconcerted. Instead he looked at his watch and then switched on the radio. It hummed and hawed for a bit and then presently the weather forecast came on. He listened intently until it was finished and was just leaning across to switch the radio off when the announcer said: 'The six o'clock news will follow in a minute and a quarter. Before the news there is a police message. There was an accident on the lower road to

133

Belling St Peter in the village of Larking, Calleshire, on Tuesday evening when a woman was knocked down and fatally injured. Will the driver of the vehicle and anyone who witnessed the accident or who may be able to give any information please telephone the Chief Constable of Calleshire, telephone Calleford 2313, or any police station.'

Henrietta gave a sudden laugh. It was high-pitched and totally devoid of humour.

'Any information!' she cried. 'That's good, isn't it? If they only knew how much information we needed . . .'

CHAPTER ELEVEN

'External examination,' Inspector Sloan began to read. 'The body was of a well-nourished female . . .'

Dr Dabbe's typewritten report of his post-mortem examination, addressed to HM Coroner for Calleshire and marked 'Copy to Chief Constable', lay on Inspector Sloan's desk. He got as far as 'aged about fifty-five' when Detective Constable Crosby came in.

'Everyone else seemed to be having tea, sir, so I brought some down. And the last of the cake.'

'Good,' said Sloan, 'I was beginning to feel the opposite of well-nourished myself. How have you got on?'

Crosby carefully carried a cup of tea across the room and sat down. Then he opened his notebook. 'The hair, sir . . .'

'Ah, yes.' Sloan fingered Dr Dabbe's report. 'I've got the name of that dye down here. All twenty-five syllables of it.'

'I found the ladies' hairdressing saloon, sir . . .'

'They drop the second "o", Constable, nowadays.'

'Really, sir? Well, she had it done at a place called "Marlene's" in the High Street. I spoke to a young person there by the name of Sandra who—er—did her.'

'When?'

'Every second Friday at ten o'clock. Without fail.'

'Yes,' Sloan set his cup down. 'It would have to be without fail. Otherwise it would show.'

'What would, sir?'

'Her fair hair. According to Dr Dabbe she was fair-haired.'

'And the girl was dark so she dyed hers dark, too,' concluded Crosby, 'so that the girl would think . . .'

'It's as good a disguise as any, too,' said Sloan. 'Especially if you don't expect it.' He paused. 'Cyril Jenkins was fair. You could see that much on the photograph.'

'Yes, sir.'

'That suggest anything to you?'

'No, sir.'

Sloan sighed. 'Constable, I agree the possibilities in this case are infinite: The murderer could be anyone, and as far as I am concerned the victim could be anyone and I am not altogether sure of the nature of the crime but there are just one or two clues worth considering.'

'Yes, sir,' said Crosby stolidly.

'The fact that Cyril Jenkins had . . .'

'Should it be "has", sir?'

Sloan glared. 'What's that? Oh, yes, that's a point.' He grunted and went on. 'Has—may have—fair hair and Grace Jenkins had fair hair which she took pains to dye the same colour as Henrietta's is interesting . . .'

'Yes, sir.'

'It's worse than drawing teeth, Crosby. Don't you have any ideas at all?'

'Yes, sir. But not about this,' he added hastily, not liking the look on Sloan's face.

'Has it occurred to you that there is one possibility that would account for it? That Cyril and Grace Jenkins were brother and sister . . .'

'No, sir,' replied Crosby truthfully. He thought for a minute and then said very cautiously, 'Where would the baby come in then?'

'I don't know.' Sloan turned back to the report. 'How did you get on otherwise?'

'No joy about where she'd been all day

136

except that it wasn't in Berebury.'

'What?'

'I showed her photograph to the inspector at the bus station. He thinks he saw her at the incoming unloading point about half-five. Doesn't know what bus she got off . . .'

'Wait a minute,' said Sloan suspiciously. 'How does he remember? That was Tuesday. Today's Friday.'

'I wondered about that, too, sir, but it seems as if an old lady tripped and fell and this Grace Jenkins helped her up and dusted her down. That sort of thing. And then handed her over to the bus people.'

Sloan nodded. 'Go on.'

'It appears she stayed in the bus station until the Larking bus left at seven-five. In the cafeteria most of the time. The waitress remembered her. Says she served her with . . .'

'Baked beans,' interposed Sloan neatly.

Crosby looked startled. 'That's right. At about . . .'

'Six o'clock,' supplied Sloan.

'How do you know, sir?'

'Not me.' Laconically. 'The pathologist. He said so. She ate them about two hours before death. That ties up with her being killed as she walked home from the last bus.'

'Wonderful, sir, isn't it, what they can do when they cut you up?'

'Yes,' said Sloan shortly.

Crosby turned back to his notebook.

'Wherever she'd been she didn't get to the bus station until after the five-fifteen to Larking had left, otherwise she'd presumably have caught that.'

'Fair enough,' agreed Sloan. 'What came in after five-fifteen and before she went into the cafeteria?'

'A great many buses,' said Crosby with feeling. 'It's about their busiest time of the day. I've got a list but I wouldn't know where to begin if it's a case of talking to conductors.'

'Return tickets?' murmured Sloan. 'They might help.'

Crosby looked doubtful. Sloan went back to the post-mortem examination report.

'Was Happy Harry any help, sir?' ventured Crosby a little later.

'Inspector Harpe,' said Sloan distantly, 'has instigated the usual routine enquiries.'

'I see, sir. Thank you, sir.'

Suddenly Sloan tapped Dr Dabbe's report. 'Get me the hospital, will you, Crosby? There's one thing I can ask the pathologist . . .'

He was put through to Dr Dabbe's office without delay. 'About this Grace Jenkins, doctor . . .'

'Yes?'

'I notice you've made a note of her blood group.'

'Routine, Inspector.'

'I know that, doctor. What I was wondering is if the blood group could help us in other

138

ways.'

'With the alleged daughter, you mean?' said Dabbe.

'Her alleged husband has turned up, too,' said Sloan; and he explained about the sighting of Cyril Jenkins.

'Blood groups aren't a way of proving maternity or paternity. Only of disproving it.'

'I don't quite follow:'

'If the child has a different one then that is a factor in sustaining evidence that it is not the child of those particular people.'

'And if it is the same?'

'That narrows the field nicely.'

'How nicely?' guardedly.

'Usually to a round ten million or so people who could be its parents.'

'I see.' Sloan thought for a moment. 'We already know that Grace Jenkins is not the mother of Henrietta . . .'

'We do.'

'But if Cyril Jenkins is alive and is the father of Henrietta, then their blood groups would tie up, wouldn't they?'

A low rumble came down the telephone line. 'First, catch your hare . . .'

*   *   *

General Sir Eustace Garwell was at home and would see Inspector C. D. Sloan.

This news was conveyed to the waiting

policemen by an elderly male retainer who had creaked to the door in answer to their ring. Sir Eustace was the fourth Garwell upon whom they had called since leaving the police station late that afternoon. The other three had numbered several Jenkins's among their acquaintance but not a Cyril Edgar nor a Grace and certainly not a Henrietta Eleanor Leslie. Nor did they look as if they could ever have had a hyphen in the family, let along a Hocklington.

It was different at 'The Laurels', Cullingoak.

Sloan and Crosby had left it until the last because it was on the way to Larking. Both the hyphen and the Hocklington would have gone quite well with the Benares brass trays and the faded Indian carpets. There were a couple of potted palms in the hall and several fronds of dusty pampas grass brushed eerily against Crosby's cheek as he and Inspector Sloan followed the man down the corridor. He walked so slowly that the two policemen had the greatest difficulty in not treading on his heels. There was that in his walk though, together with the fact that he had referred to 'the General' and not 'Sir Eustace', that made Sloan say, 'You've seen service yourself?'

'Batman to the General, sir, since he was a subaltern.'

'The West Calleshires or the Cavalry?' hazarded Sloan.

140

The man stopped in his tracks and drew himself up to his full height. 'The East Calleshires, sir, not the West.'

Sloan began to feel hopeful.

'We only live in the western part of the county,' went on the man, 'because her ladyship was left this property, and though she's been dead some years, the General's too old to be making a change.'

'I'm sorry,' said Sloan, suitably abject.

A very old gentleman struggled out of a chair as they entered.

'Come in, gentlemen, come in. It's not often I have any callers in the evening. We live a very quiet life here, you know. Stopped going out when m'wife died. What'll you take to drink?'

Sloan declined port, madeira and brandy in that order.

'On duty, sir, I'm afraid.'

The General nodded sympathetically, and said they would forgive him his brandy and soda because he wasn't on duty any more, in fact it was many a long year now since he had been.

'It's about the past we've come,' said Sloan by way of making a beginning.

'My memory's not what it used to be,' said the old man.

'Pity,' murmured Crosby *sotto voce*.

'What's that? I can't hear so well either. Damned MO fellow wants me to have a hearing aid thing. Can't be bothered.' The

General indicated a chair on his left and said to Sloan, 'If you would sit here I shall hear you better.' He settled himself back in his own chair. 'Ah, that's more comfortable. Now, how far back in the past do you want to go? Ladysmith?'

'Ladysmith?' echoed Sloan, considerably startled.

'It was Mafeking they made all the fuss about—they forgot the siege of Ladysmith.' He fixed Sloan with a bleary eye. 'Do you want to know about Ladysmith?'

'You were there, sir?'

The General gave a deep chuckle. 'I was there. I was there for a long time. The whole siege. And I've never wasted a drop of drink or a morsel of food since.' He leant forward. 'Are you sure about that brandy?'

'Certainly, sir. Thank you.'

The General took another sip. 'Commissioned in '99. Went through the whole of the Boer War. Nearly died of fever more than once. Still,' he brightened, 'none of it seemed to do me any harm.'

This much, at least, was patently true. They were looking at a very old man indeed but he seemed to be in possession of all his faculties. Sloan thought back quickly, dredging through his schoolboy memory for names of battles.

'Were you at Omdurman, Sir Eustace?'

Sir Eustace Garwell waved the brandy glass under his nose with a thin hand, sniffing appreciatively. The veins on his hand stood out, hard and gnarled. 'No, sir, I was not at Omdurman. Incredible as it may seem now, I was too young for that episode in our military history. At the time I was very distressed about missing it by a year or so. I was foolish enough to fear that there weren't going to be any more wars.' He gave a melancholy snort. 'I needn't have worried, need I?'

'No, sir . . .'

'Now, on the whole I'm rather glad. You realise, don't you, that had I been born a couple of years earlier I should probably be dead by now.'

Sloan took a moment or two to work this out and then he said, 'I see what you mean, sir.'

'The East Callies were there, of course. Battle honours and all that . . .'

'Yes.' Sloan raised his voice a little. 'There is just one little matter on which you may be able to help us by remembering. After Ladysmith. Probably sometime between the wars.'

'I was in India from '04 to 1913,' said the General helpfully. 'In the Punjab.'

'Not those wars,' said Sloan hastily, hoping Sir Eustace was too deaf to have heard Crosby's snort. 'Between the other two.'

'Ah. It wasn't the same, you know.'

'I daresay not,' said Sloan dryly.

'Everything changed after 1914 but war most of all.'

143

'Do you recollect a Sergeant Jenkins in the Regiment, sir?'

There was a row of ivory elephants on the mantelpiece, their trunks properly facing the door. Sloan had time to count them before the General replied.

'Jenkins did you say? No, the name doesn't mean anything to me. Known quite a few men of that name in m'time but not in the Regiment. Hirst might know. Ask him.'

'Thank you, sir, I will.'

'They put me on the Staff,' said the old voice querulously. 'You never know anyone then.'

'Did you ever have a woman called Grace Jenkins working for you either, sir?'

'Can't say that we did. We had a housekeeper but she's been dead for years and her name wasn't Jenkins.'

'Or Wright?'

'No. One of the cleaning women might have been called that. You'd have to ask Hirst. They come and go, you know.'

If the dust on the ivory elephants was any measure, this was one of the times when they had gone.

'No, not a cleaning woman,' said Sloan. 'A children's nurse, perhaps. A nanny?'

'Never had any children,' said the General firmly. 'No nannies about the place ever.'

'I see, sir. Thank you. Well, then, I must apologise for disturbing you. Routine enquiry,

144

you understand.'

'Quite so.'

Sloan got up to go. 'About a woman who used to work as a children's nurse for a family called Hocklington-Garwell and we're trying to trace . . .'

Without any warning the whole atmosphere inside the drawing-room of 'The Laurels', Cullingoak, changed.

Two beady eyes peered at Sloan over the top of the brandy glass. Just as quickly the old face became suffused with colour. A choleric General Sir Eustace Garwell put down his glass with shaking hands.

'Sir,' he said, quite outraged, 'is this a joke?'

He struggled to his feet, anger in every feature of his stiff and ancient frame. He tottered over to the wall and put his finger on a bell.

'If I were a younger man, sir,' he quavered, 'I would send for a horse-whip. As it is, I shall just ask my man to show you the door. Goodnight, sir, goodnight.'

CHAPTER TWELVE

As always, Sloan was polite.

He had long ago learned that there were few situations where a police officer—or anyone else, for that matter—gained by not being.

Henrietta was sitting opposite him and Crosby in the little parlour of Boundary Cottage.

'Yes, Inspector. I'm certain it was Hocklington-Garwell. It's not really a name you could confuse, is it?'

'No, miss, that's very true.'

'Besides, why should I tell you a name like that if it isn't the one I was told?'

'That's not for me to say, miss.'

She stared at him. 'You do believe me, don't you?'

'The mention of the name certainly upset the old gentleman, miss. He ordered us out of the house.'

Henrietta looked puzzled. 'I can't understand it at all. It was Hocklington-Garwell and they had two boys. Master Michael and Master Hugo. I heard such a lot about them always . . .'

'The General said he hadn't had any children,' said Sloan.

'There you are, then. It must have been the wrong man . . .'

'But the merest mention of the name upset him, miss. There was no mistake about that.'

She subsided again, shaking her head. 'I can't begin to explain that. They're wrong, you know, when they say "What's in a name?". There seems to be everything in it.'

'Just at the moment,' agreed Sloan. He

coughed. 'About the other matter, miss . . .

'My father?'

'The man in the photograph.'

'Cyril Jenkins . . .'

'Yes, miss. We've got a general call out for him now, starting in the Calleford area . . .'

'You'll find him, won't you?'

'I think we will,' said Sloan with a certain amount of reservation. 'Whether, if we do, we shall find he fulfils all three conditions of identity . . .'

'Three?'

'That your father, the man in the photograph and Cyril Edgar Jenkins are all one and the same.'

She nodded and said positively, 'I can only tell you one of them, that he was the man in the photograph.' She tightened her lips. 'You'll have to tell me the other two afterwards, won't you?'

Sloan frowned. There were quite a few little matters that Cyril Jenkins could inform them about and the first question they would ask him was where exactly he had been just before eight o'clock on Tuesday evening. Aloud he said, 'We'll tell you all we can, miss, though you realise someone might simply have borrowed his photograph to put on the mantelpiece here?'

She smiled wanly. 'Is that what they call a father figure, Inspector?'

'Something like that, miss.'

'Why should she have told me he was dead if he wasn't?'

'I don't know, miss.' Sloan couldn't remember a time when he had used the phrase so often. 'He might have left her, I suppose . . .' It wasn't a subject he was prepared to pursue at this moment, so he cleared his throat and said, 'In view of what you have told us about the War Memorial and the Rector about the medals, we are in touch with the War Office but there will inevitably be a little delay.'

A brief smile flitted across her face and was gone. 'Friday afternoon's not the best time, is it?'

'No, miss. I doubt if we shall have anything in time for the inquest.'

'Mr Arbican's coming,' she said, 'and he's going to get someone to start going through the Court Adoption records.'

'That's a long job,' said Sloan, who had already taken advice on this point.

'Starting with the Calleshire County Court and the Berebury, Luston and Calleford Magistrates' ones. That's the most hopeful, isn't it?' she said. 'I expect you think I'm being unreasonable, Inspector, but I must know who I am—even if Bill Thorpe doesn't care.'

'Doesn't he?' said Sloan alertly.

She grimaced. 'He only thinks it's important if you happen to be an Aberdeen Angus bull.'

*   *   *

'Back to Berebury?' enquired Crosby hopefully, as they left Boundary Cottage. Breakfast was the only solid meal he had had so far that day and he was getting increasingly aware of the fact.

Sloan got into the car beside him. 'No.' He got out his notebook. 'So young Thorpe doesn't care who she is . . .'

'So she said.'

'But he still wants to marry her.'

'That's right,' said Crosby, who privately found it rather romantic.

'Has it occurred to you that that could be because he already knows who she is?'

'No,' responded Crosby simply.

'I think,' said Sloan, 'we shall have to look into the background of young Mr Thorpe. Just to be on the safe side, you might say.'

'Now?' Crosby started up the engine.

'No. Later. Just drive up the road. We're going to call at The Hall. To see what Mr James Hibbs knows.'

Mr and Mrs Hibbs were just finishing their evening meal. Enough of its aroma still hung about to tantalise Crosby's idle digestive juices, though there was no sign of food. The Hibbs were having coffee by a log fire in their hall, the two gun dogs supine before it. A bare wooden staircase clambered up to the first floor. The rest was dark panelling and the total effect was of great comfort.

Sloan declined coffee out of cups so tiny and fragile-looking that he could not bear to think of them in Constable Crosby's hands.

'You're quite sure?' said Mrs Hibbs. She was a tall, imposing woman with a deep voice. 'Or would you prefer some beer?'

Sloan—to say nothing of Crosby—would have greatly preferred some beer but he shook his head regretfully. 'Thank you, no madam. We just want to ask a few more questions about the late Mrs Grace Jenkins.'

'A terrible business,' said Mrs Hibbs. 'To think of her lying there in the road all night, and nobody knew.'

'Except, I daresay,' put in Hibbs, 'the fellow who knocked her down. All my eye, you know, this business that you can say you didn't notice the bump. Any driver would notice.'

'Quite so, sir.'

'It's a wonder that James didn't find her himself,' went on Mrs Hibbs, placidly pouring out more coffee.

'Really, madam?'

'You sometimes take Richard and Berengaria that way, don't you, dear?'

'Yes,' said Hibbs rather shortly.

Sloan said, 'Who?'

'Richard and Berengaria.' She pointed to the dogs. 'We always call them after kings and queens, you know.'

'I see, madam.' Sloan, who thought dogs should be called 'Spot' or 'Lassie', turned to

James Hibbs. 'Did you happen to take them that way on Tuesday, sir?'

'No, Inspector.'

'Which way,' mildly, 'did you take them?'

'Towards the village. I had some letters to post.'

'About what time would that have been?'

'Half-past eight-ish.'

'And you saw nothing and nobody?' The answer to that anyway was a foregone conclusion.

'No.'

'I see, sir. Thank you.' Sloan changed his tone and said easily, 'We're running into a little difficulty in establishing the girl's antecedents . . . it wouldn't matter so much if Henrietta—Miss Jenkins—weren't under twenty-one.'

'Probate, I suppose,' said Hibbs wisely. 'And she was intestate, too, I daresay. I'm forever advising people to make their wills but they won't, you know. They think they're immortal.'

'Quite so, sir,' said Sloan, who hadn't made his own just yet.

'She needn't worry about the cottage, if that's on her mind. She's a protected tenant and anyway I can't see myself putting her on the street.'

This was obviously meant to be a mild joke, for his wife smiled.

'Even if Threlkeld would advise it,' went on Hibbs heartily, 'and I expect he would. There's

151

more to being an agent than that.'

'That letter he found for us,' said Sloan, 'which put us on to the Calleford solicitors . . .'

'Yes?'

'It didn't get us much further. They had no records of any dealings with her.'

'I'm not really surprised,' said Hibbs. 'It was a long time ago.'

'That's true.' Sloan, it seemed, was all affability and agreement. 'Actually, we have gone a bit further back than that. To some people Grace Jenkins used to work for . . .'

'Really?' Hibbs didn't sound unduly interested.

'They were called Hocklington-Garwell.'

'Yes?' His face was a mask of polite interest.

'Does the name convey anything to you?'

Hibbs frowned. 'Can't say it does, Inspector.'

But it did to Mrs Hibbs.

Sloan could see that from her face.

*   *   *

Superintendent Leeyes was never in a very good mood first thing in the morning. He sent for Inspector Sloan as soon as he got to the police station on the Saturday morning. The portents were not good.

'Well, Sloan, any news?'

'Not very much, sir. Inspector Harpe hasn't got anything for us at all on the Traffic side.

No response at all to the radio appeal. Of course, it's early days yet—it only went out last night.'

Leeyes grunted. 'They either saw it or they didn't see it.'

'No witnesses,' went on Sloan hastily. 'No cars taken in for suspicious repairs anywhere in the county . . .'

'I don't know what we have a Traffic Division for,' grumbled Leeyes.

Sloan kept silent.

'What about Somerset House?'

'Still searching, sir.'

Leeyes grunted again. 'And the pensions people?'

'They've been on the 'phone. They say they're paying out a total disability pension to a Cyril Edgar Jenkins . . .'

'Oh?'

'Not him. This one was wounded on the Somme in July 1916.'

'That's not a lot of help.'

'No, sir.' He coughed. 'In view of the brief reappearance of Jenkins I've asked the War Office to turn up the Calleshire Regiment records. His discharge papers would be a help.'

'So would his appearance,' said Leeyes briskly. 'Calleford haven't found him yet, I take it?'

'I rang them this morning,' said Sloan obliquely. 'They'd visited all the people called Jenkins in the city itself without finding anyone corresponding to either the photograph or the girl's description—but there's a big hinterland to Calleford. And it was their market-day yesterday, too. He might have come in to that—or to shop or to work.'

'Or to see the Minster,' suggested Leeyes sarcastically. 'What I don't like about it is the coincidence.'

'I suppose it is odd,' conceded Sloan. 'The one day the girl happens to go there she sees him.'

'She says she sees him,' snapped Leeyes.

'On the other hand he might be there every day. For all we know he is.'

'Get anywhere with the Garwells?' Superintendent Leeyes always changed his ground rather than be forced into a conclusion which might subsequently turn out to be incorrect. His subordinates rarely caught him out—even if they never realised why it was.

Sloan obediently told him how far he had got with the Garwells.

Leeyes sniffed. 'Funny, that.'

'Yes, sir. The General very nearly threw a fit and Mrs Hibbs knew something. I'm sure of that.'

'What about Hibbs himself?'

'Didn't move a muscle. If the name meant anything to him, it didn't show in his face like it did in hers.'

'Is he putting the girl out?' said Leeyes hopefully. 'That might mean something.'

'No,' Sloan shook his head. 'He says she's a protected tenant but in any case he wouldn't.'

'Why not?'

'It's still a bit feudal out there, sir.'

'They had this sort of trouble in feudal times.'

'Gave me the impression, sir, that he feels a bit responsible for his tenants.'

'Impression be blowed,' retorted Leeyes vigorously. 'What we want to know is whether he was literally responsible for the girl. Biologically speaking.'

'Quite so,' murmured Sloan weakly.

'It's all very well for him to be hinting that he couldn't put her on the street because it wasn't expected of a man in his position but,' Leeyes glared, 'that's as good a way of concealing a real stake in her welfare as any.'

'Sort of taking a fatherly interest?' suggested Sloan.

The Superintendent snorted. 'This village patriarch of yours—what's his wife like?'

'Tall, what you might call a commanding presence.'

Leeyes looked interested. He felt he had one of those himself.

'She didn't,' said Sloan cautiously, 'strike me as the sort of woman to overlook even one wild oat.'

'There you are then.' He veered away from the subject of Hibbs's as quickly as he had brought it up. 'What next?'

'The inquest is in an hour.' Sloan looked at his watch. 'And then a few inquiries about young Master Thorpe of Shire Oak Farm.'

'Oh?' Leeyes's head came up like a hound just offered a new scent.

'He,' said Sloan meaningfully, 'doesn't care who she is. He just wants to marry her as soon as possible. That may only be love's young dream . . .'

'Ahah,' the Superintendent leered at Sloan. 'From what you've said she's a mettlesome girl.'

'. . . on the other hand,' said Sloan repressively, 'it may not.'

*   *   *

The Rector of Larking and Mrs Meyton and Bill Thorpe all went into Berebury with Henrietta for the inquest. It was to be held in the Town Hall and they met Felix Arbican, the solicitor, about half an hour beforehand in one of the numerous rooms leading off the main hall.

'I can't predict the outcome,' was the first thing Arbican said to them after shaking hands gravely. 'You may get a verdict of death by misadventure. You may get an adjournment.'

'Oh, dear,' said Henrietta.

'The police may want more time to find the driver of the car . . .'

'And Cyril Jenkins.'

Arbican started. 'Who?'

Henrietta told him about the previous afternoon.

'I'm very glad to hear you've seen him,' responded the solicitor. 'It would seem at this juncture that a little light on the proceedings would be a great help.'

'No light was shed,' said Henrietta austerely.

'None?'

'We couldn't find him in the crowd,' said Bill Thorpe.

Arbican turned to Thorpe and asked shrewdly, 'Were you able to identify him?'

Bill Thorpe shook his head. 'I only saw his back.'

'I see. So Miss Jenkins is the only person who is certain who it was and the police haven't yet found him?'

'Yes,' intervened Henrietta tersely.

'Extraordinary business altogether.'

'More extraordinary than that,' said Mr Meyton, and told him about the medals.

Arbican's limpid gaze fell upon the Rector. 'Most peculiar. Let us hope that the police are able to find this man and that when they do some—er—satisfactory explanation is forthcoming.' He coughed. 'In the meantime I think we had better come back to the more immediate matter of the inquest.'

Henrietta lifted her face expectantly. The animation which had been there since she saw

Cyril Jenkins had gone.

'Your part, Miss Jenkins, is quite simple. You have only to establish identity.'

'Quite simple!' she echoed bitterly. 'It's anything but simple.'

'To establish identity as you knew it,' amplified Arbican. 'If the police have evidence that Grace Jenkins was not—er—Grace Jenkins they will bring it. As far as you are concerned that has always been the name by which you knew her . . .'

'Yes.'

'Strong presumptive evidence. In any case . . .'

'Yes?'

'The Coroner holds an inquest on a body, not—so to speak—on a person. An unknown body sometimes.'

'I see.'

'His duty will be to establish the cause of death. If it was from other than natural causes, and it—um—appears to have been, then he has a parallel duty to inquire into the nature of the cause.'

'I see.' Henrietta wasn't really listening any more. For one thing, she found it difficult to concentrate now. Her mind wandered off so easily that she couldn't keep all her attention on what someone was saying. For another she didn't really want to hear a legal lecture from a prosperous-looking man in a black suit. He had never had cause to wonder who he was.

He was too confident for that.

'The cause of death,' he was saying didactically, 'would appear to be obvious. The main point must be the identity of the driver. If the police found him we could try suing for damages.'

'Damages?'

'Substantial damages,' said Arbican.

'If no one else saw the car even, let alone the driver, I don't see how they'll ever find him.'

Bill Thorpe was getting restive too. 'And it was nearly a week ago already.'

'They'll go on trying,' said the solicitor. 'They're very persistent.'

'You say,' put in Mrs Meyton anxiously, 'that all Henrietta will have to do will be to give evidence of identification?'

'That's all, Mrs Meyton. It won't take very long. The Coroner may want to know if Mrs Jenkins's sight and hearing were normal. If it seems relevant her doctor could be called in as an expert witness on the point. Otherwise the Coroner will just note what she says.'

' "Write that down," the King said,' burbled Henrietta hysterically, ' "and reduce the answer to shillings and pence." '

Arbican looked bewildered.

'Alice in Wonderland,' said the Rector as if that explained everything.

CHAPTER THIRTEEN

There was a sudden stir and a rustle of feet. Seven men filed into the room where the inquest was being held and sat together at one side of the dais. Henrietta looked at Arbican.

'The jury, Miss Jenkins.'

She hadn't known there would be a jury.

'There is always a jury when death is caused by a vehicle on a public highway.'

The Rector counted them. 'I thought juries were like apostles . . .'

Arbican frowned. 'I beg your pardon?'

'Twelve in number.'

'Not for a Coroner's Inquest.'

'So We Are Seven?'

Arbican frowned again. 'We are seven?'

'It's another quotation,' said Mr Meyton kindly.

Henrietta was the first person to be called. A man handed her a Bible and told her what to say.

'I hereby swear by Almighty God that the evidence I shall give touching the death of Grace Edith Jenkins shall be the truth, the whole truth and nothing but the truth.'

The Coroner picked up his pen. 'Your name?'

She swallowed visibly. 'Henrietta Eleanor Leslie Jenkins.'

'You have seen the body declared to be that of a woman found on the lower road to Belling St Peter in the village of Larking on Wednesday morning last?'

'Yes.'

'A little louder please, Miss Jenkins.'

'Yes.'

'And you identify it as that of Grace Edith Jenkins?'

'I do.'

'What was your relationship to the deceased?'

She stared at a spot on the wall above and behind the Coroner's head and said faintly, 'Adopted daughter.'

The Coroner twitched his papers. 'I must ask you to speak up. I am aware that this must perforce be a painful occasion to you but an inquest is a public enquiry, and the public have a right, if not a duty, to hear what is said.'

'Adopted daughter.' She said it more firmly this time, as if she herself were more sure.

'Thank you.' His courtesy was automatic, without sarcasm. 'When did you last see the deceased alive?'

'Early in January, before I went back to university.' She hesitated. 'I was due home at the end of this month but, of course . . .' her voice trailed away.

'Quite so.' The Coroner made a further note on his papers. 'That will be all for the time being, Miss Jenkins. I must ask you to remain in the building as you may be recalled later.'

Harry Ford, postman, came next, and deposed how he had come across the body early on Wednesday morning.

Graphically.

Mrs Callows described how Mrs Jenkins had got off the last bus with her and Mrs Perkins.

Melodramatically.

Then PC Hepple related that which he had found.

Technically.

The Coroner wrote down the width of the carriageway and said, 'And the length of the skid mark?'

Hepple cleared his throat. 'I'm sorry, sir, I'm afraid there wasn't one.'

The Coroner was rather like a rook. An elderly but still spry rook. And very alert. He didn't miss the fact that there was no evidence of the car's brakes being urgently applied. Nor did he comment on it. Henrietta moved a little forward on her chair as if she hadn't quite heard the constable properly but otherwise his statement made no visible impact.

Then a tall thin man was taking the oath with practised ease. He identified himself—though the Coroner must have known him well—as Hector Smithson Dabbe, Bachelor of Medicine and Bachelor of Surgery, Consultant Pathologist to the Berebury Group Hospital

Management Committee. Then he gave his evidence.

Impersonally.

Henrietta lowered her head as if in defence but she couldn't escape the pathologist's voice while he explained that, in his opinion, the injuries sustained by the body which he was given to understand was that of one Grace Edith Jenkins . . .

Henrietta noticed the word 'which'. Grace Jenkins was—had been—a person. She wasn't any longer. This man had said 'which' not 'who'.

'. . . were consistent,' said Dr Dabbe, 'with her having been run over by a heavy vehicle twice.'

Henrietta felt sick.

The Coroner thanked Dr Dabbe and then shuffled his papers into order and looked at the jury. 'I am required by law to adjourn an inquest for fourteen days if I am requested to do so by the Chief Constable on the grounds that a person may be charged with murder, manslaughter or with causing death by reckless or dangerous driving.'

He paused. Someone in the room sneezed into the stillness.

'I have received such a request from the Chief Constable of Calleshire and this inquest is accordingly adjourned for two weeks. No doubt the Press will take cognisance of the fact that the police are appealing for witnesses.'

The Press—in the person of a ginger-haired cub reporter from the *Berebury News*—obediently scribbled a note and suddenly it was all over.

*   *   *

Inspector Sloan came up to Henrietta. 'I won't keep you, miss. There's just one thing I must say to you.'

'Yes?'

'I know you weren't thinking of it but I must formally ask you not to go abroad before the inquest is resumed.'

She smiled wanly. 'I promise.'

He hesitated. 'May I hazard a guess, miss, that you've never been abroad at all?'

'Never, Inspector. How did you know?'

He didn't answer directly. 'Did you ever want to?'

'Yes, I did. Especially lately. Since I've been at university, I mean. Some friends went on a reading party to France last summer. They asked me to go with them and I should have liked to have gone . . .'

'But Grace Jenkins didn't want you to . . .' put in Sloan.

'That's right. How did you know?'

'Did she say why?'

'I thought it was because of the money.'

'It may have been, miss, but there could have been another reason too.'

'Could there?' It was impossible to tell if she was interested or not.

'To go abroad you need a passport.'

'Yes . . .'

'To get a passport you need a birth certificate.'

She was quicker to follow him than he expected, swooping down on the point. 'That means I'm not Jenkins, doesn't it?'

'I think so.'

'Otherwise,' went on Henrietta slowly, 'she could have arranged it all without my actually seeing the birth certificate.'

'Probably.'

'But not if my surname wasn't Jenkins.'

'No.'

They stood a moment in silence then Henrietta said, 'I shall have to sign my name somewhere sometime . . .'

'I should stick to Jenkins for the time being,' advised Sloan.

'A living lie?'

'Call it a working compromise.'

'Or shall I just make my mark?'

'Your mark, miss?'

'I think an "X" would be most appropriate.' She gave him a wintry smile. 'After all, it does stand for the unknown quantity as well as the illiterate.'

He opened his mouth to answer but she forestalled him.

'There's one thing anyway . . .'

'Yes, miss?'

'I'm practically certain of a place in any college team you care to mention.'

'College team?' echoed Sloan, momentarily bewildered.

'There's always an A.N. Other there, you know,' she said swiftly. And was gone.

* * *

'That's that,' observed Crosby without enthusiasm as he and Inspector Sloan got back to the police station afterwards. 'We've only got two weeks and we still don't know what sort of a car or where to look for the driver.'

'One good thing though,' said Sloan, determinedly cheerful. 'From what the Coroner said everyone will think we're looking for a dangerous driver.'

Crosby sniffed. 'Needle in a haystack, more like. PC Hepple said to tell you there's nothing new at his end. He can't find anyone who saw or heard a car on Tuesday evening.'

'No.' Sloan was not altogether surprised. 'No, I reckon whoever killed her sat and waited in the car park of the pub and then just timed her walk from the bus stop to the bad corner.'

'That's a bit chancy,' objected Crosby. 'She might not have been on that bus.'

'I think,' gently, 'that he knew she was on it. The only real risk was that someone else from

166

down the lane might have been on it too. But now I've seen how few houses there are there, I don't think that was anything to worry about.' He pushed open his office door, and crossed over to his desk. There was a message lying there for him. 'Hullo, the Army have answered. Read this, Crosby.'

'Jenkins, C. E. Sergeant, The East Calleshires,' read Crosby aloud. 'Enlisted September, 1939, demobilised July, 1946. Address on enlistment . . .'

'Go on.'

'Holly Tree Farm,' said Crosby slowly, 'Rooden Parva, Near Calleford.'

'The plot thickens,' said Sloan, rubbing his hands.

'That's what the girl told us, wasn't it, sir? Holly Tree Farm.'

'That's right. She said she didn't know the second bit.' He paused. 'Get me the Calleford police . . .'

Sloan spoke to someone on duty there, waited an appreciable time while the listener looked something up and finally thanked him and replaced the receiver.

Crosby stood poised between the door and the desk. 'Are we going there, sir?'

'Not straight. We're calling somewhere on the way. They've looked up the address. There's no one called Jenkins there now. Walsh is the name of the occupier.' Sloan looked at his watch. 'It's nearly twelve. Do you suppose Hirst nips out for a quick one before lunch?'

'Hirst?' said Crosby blankly.

'The General's man. We must know what's so sinister about the magic words Hocklington-Garwell.'

Which was how Detective Inspector Sloan and Detective Constable Crosby came to be enjoying a pint of beer at 'The Bull' in Cullingoak shortly after half-past twelve. The bar was comfortably full.

'He usually comes in for a few minutes,' agreed the landlord on enquiry. 'He's got the old gentleman, see. Got to give him his lunch at quarter-past. Very particular about time, is the General. Same in the evening. He can't come out till he's got him settled for the night.' He swept the two plain-clothes men with an appraising glance. 'You friends of his?'

'Sort of,' agreed Sloan non-committally.

The landlord leaned two massive elbows on the bar. 'If it's money you're after you can collect it somewhere else. I'm not having anyone dunned in my house.'

'No,' said Sloan distantly. 'We're not after money.'

'That's all right then,' said the landlord.

Sloan allowed a suitable pause before asking, 'Horses or dogs?'

The landlord swept up a couple of empty glasses from the bar with arms too brawny for such light work. 'Horses. Nothing much—just the odd flutter—like they all do.'

'Did he come in last night?'

'Hirst?' The landlord frowned. 'Now you come to mention it, I don't think he did. Perhaps his old gentleman wanted him. He's not young, isn't the General.'

'Quite,' agreed Sloan. 'What'll you have?'

It was nearly ten to one before Hirst appeared. He came in quietly, a newspaper— open at the sporting page—tucked under his arm. He looked a little younger in the pub than he had done in the General's house, but not much. His shoes were polished to perfection and his hair neatly plastered down but he, like his master, was showing signs of advancing age. Sloan let him get his pint and sit down before he looked in his direction.

'I fear, Hirst, that I upset the General last night,' he said.

Hirst looked up, recognised him and put down his glass with a hand that was not quite steady. 'Yes, sir. That you did.'

'It was quite accidental . . .'

'Proper upset, he was. I had quite a time with him last night after you'd gone, I can tell you.'

'You did?' enquired Sloan, even more interested.

'Carrying on alarming he was till I got him to bed.'

'Hirst, what was it we said that did it?'

'The General didn't say.' He lifted his glass.

'But he was upset all right.'

'I was asking him something about the past,' said Sloan carefully, watching Hirst's face. 'Something I wanted to know about a woman who—I think—was called Grace Jenkins.'

There was no reaction from Hirst.

'Do you know the name?' persisted Sloan.

'Can't say that I do.' Reassured, he took another pull at his beer. 'It's a common enough one.'

'That's part of the trouble.'

'I see.'

'Garwell's not a common name,' said Sloan conversationally.

'No,' agreed Hirst. 'There's not many of them about.'

'And Hocklington-Garwell isn't common at all.'

Hirst set his glass down with a clatter. 'You mentioned Hocklington-Garwell to the General?'

'I did.'

'You shouldn't have done that, sir,' said Hirst reproachfully.

'This woman Jenkins told her daughter that she used to be nursemaid to the family.'

'No wonder the General was so upset. In fact, what with her ladyship being dead, I should say it would have upset the General more than anything else would have done.'

'It did,' agreed Sloan briefly, 'but why?'

Hirst sucked his teeth. 'Begging your

pardon, Mr Sloan, sir, I should have said it was all over and done with long before your time.'

'What,' cried Sloan in exasperation, 'was all over and done with before my time?'

'That explains why the General was so upset about your being a detective, sir, if you'll forgive my mentioning it.'

Sloan, who had been a detective for at least ten years without ever before feeling the fact to be unmentionable, looked at the faded gentleman's gentleman and said he would forgive him.

'I kept on telling him,' said Hirst, 'that it was all over and done with.' He took another sip of beer. 'But it wasn't any good. I had to get the doctor to him this morning, you know.'

'Hirst,' said Sloan dangerously, 'I need to know exactly what it was that was over and done with before my time and I need to know now.'

'The Hocklington-Garwell business. Before the last war, it was. And she is dead now, God rest her soul, so why drag it up again?'

'Who is dead?' Sloan was hanging on to his temper with an effort. A great effort.

'Her ladyship, like I told you. And Major Hocklington, too, for all I know.'

'Hirst, I think I am beginning to see daylight. Hocklington and Garwell are two different people, aren't they?'

'That's right, sir. Like I said. There's the General who you saw yesterday and then there was Major Hocklington—only it's all a long time ago now, sir, so can't you let the whole business alone?'

'Not as easily as you might think, Hirst.'

'For the sake of the General, sir . . .'

'Am I to understand, Hirst, that Lady Garwell and this Major Hocklington had an affair?'

Hirst plunged his face into the pint glass as far as it would go and was understood to say that that was about the long and short of it.

Detective Inspector Sloan let out a great shout of laughter.

'Please, sir,' begged Hirst. 'Not here in a public bar. The General wouldn't like it.'

'No,' agreed Sloan. 'I can see now why he didn't like my asking him if he was called Hocklington-Garwell. In the circumstances, I'm not sure that I would have cared for it myself. Would a note of apology help?'

'It might, sir.' Hirst sounded grateful. 'But why did you do it, sir? It's all such a long time ago now. We never had any children in the family, sir, so we never had any nursemaid at all. And there's no call for a nursemaid without babies to look after, is there?'

'I asked him, Hirst, because a woman, who is also dead now, had a sense of humour.'

'Really, sir?' Hirst was polite but sounded unconvinced.

'Yes, Hirst, really. I never met her but I am coming to know her quite well. She misled me

172

at first but I think I am beginning to understand her now.'

'Indeed, sir?'

'A very interesting woman. Give me your glass, will you?'

'Thank you, sir. I don't mind if I do.'

* * *

The Rector of Larking and Mrs Meyton joined Henrietta as soon as the inquest was over. She was standing talking to Bill Thorpe and Arbican.

'There is very little more you can do at this stage, Miss Jenkins,' the solicitor was saying. 'You must, of course, be available for the adjourned inquest.'

'I shan't run away.' Henrietta sounded as if she had had enough of life for one morning.

'Of course not,' pacifically. 'And then there will be the question of intestacy.'

'What does that mean?'

Mr Meyton coughed. 'I think that is the greatest virtue of education . . .'

Arbican turned politely to the Rector, who said, 'You learn the importance of admitting you don't know.'

'Quite so.' Arbican turned back to Henrietta. 'Grace Jenkins appears to have died without making a will. That is to say . . .' (legal-fashion, he qualified the statement immediately) '. . . we cannot find one. It hasn't

173

been deposited with the bank, nor presumably with any Berebury solicitor. . .'

'How do you know that?' asked Bill Thorpe.

'There is a fairly full account of the accident in yesterday's local newspaper. I think any Berebury firm holding such a will would have made themselves known by now.'

'The bureau,' said Henrietta heavily. 'I expect it was in the bureau.'

There was a little silence. They had nearly forgotten the bureau.

Arbican coughed. 'In the meantime, I think perhaps the best course of action would be . . .'

'I think,' Bill Thorpe interrupted him firmly, 'that the best course of action would be for me to marry Henrietta as quickly as possible.'

CHAPTER FOURTEEN

Rooden Parva was really little more than a hamlet.

It lay in the farthest corner of the county, south of Calleford and south of the much more substantial village of Great Rooden. Sloan and Crosby got there at about half-past two when the calm of a country Saturday afternoon had descended on a scene that could never have been exactly lively.

'This is a dead-and-alive hole, all right,' said Crosby. They had pulled up at the only garage

174

in Rooden Parva to ask the way and Crosby had pushed a bell marked 'For Service' beside the solitary petrol pump.

Nothing whatsoever happened.

'Try the shop,' suggested Sloan tetchily.

They were luckier there. Crosby came out smelling faintly of paraffin and said Holly Tree Farm was about a mile and a half out in the country.

'This being Piccadilly Circus, I suppose,' said Sloan, looking at all of twelve houses clustered together.

'They said we can't miss it,' said Crosby. 'There's only one road anyway.'

Holly Tree Farm lay at the end of the road. It, too, had fallen into a sort of rural torpor, though this appeared to be a permanent state and in no way connected with its being Saturday afternoon. The front door, dimly visible behind a barricade of holly trees, looked as if it hadn't been opened in years. Knocking on the back door alerted a few hens that were pecking about in the yard but nothing and nobody else. The farmhouse was old, a long low building with windows designed to keep out the light and a back door built for small men.

They turned their attention to the yard. A long barn lay on the left, its thatched roof proving fertile ground for all manner of vegetation. Beyond was a sinister little shed about whose true function Sloan was in no

175

doubt at all. Two elderly tractors stood in another corner beside a rusty implement whose nature was obscure to the two town-bred policemen.

'Is that a harrow?' asked Crosby uncertainly.

'I'd put it in the Chamber of Horrors if it was mine,' began Sloan when suddenly they were not alone any more.

A woman wearing an old raincoat emerged cautiously from behind the barn.

'Are you from the Milk Marketing Board?' she called, keeping her distance.

Sloan said they were not.

She advanced a little.

'The Ministry of Agriculture?'

Sloan shook his head and she came nearer still.

'No,' she said ambiguously, 'I can see you're not from them.' She had a weather-beaten face, burnt by sun and wind, and she could have been almost any age at all. Besides her old raincoat, she had on a serge skirt and black Wellington boots. 'We paid the rates . . .'

There were no visitors at Holly Tree Farm it seemed, save official ones. Sloan explained that he was looking for a man called Cyril Jenkins.

'Jenkins,' she repeated vaguely. 'Not here. There's just me and Walsh here.'

'Now,' agreed Sloan. 'But once there were Jenkins's here.'

Her face cleared. 'That's right. Afore us.'

'Splendid,' said Sloan warmly. 'Now, do you know what became of them?'

'The old chap died,' she said. 'Before our time. We've been here twenty years, you know.'

Sloan didn't doubt it. It was certainly twenty years since anyone had repaired the barn roof.

'We got it off the old chap,' she said. 'The young 'un didn't seem to want it.'

'The young 'un?' Sloan strove to hide his interest.

'Yes.' She looked at him curiously. 'He didn't want it. He'd been away, you know, in the war.'

'That's right.'

'Didn't seem as if he could settle afterwards. Not here.'

Sloan could well believe it. Aloud he said, 'It isn't easy if you've been away for any time.'

'No.' She stood considering the two men. 'Times, it's a bit quiet at Holly Tree, you know. There's just Walsh and me. Still, we don't want for nothing and that's something.'

It wasn't strictly true. A bath wouldn't have been out of place as far as Mrs Walsh was concerned. Say, once a month . . .

'This young 'un,' said Sloan. 'Did he ever marry?'

She nodded her head. 'Yes, but I did hear tell his wife died.'

'Where did they go after you came here?' It

was the question which counted and for a moment Sloan thought she was going to say she didn't know.

Instead she frowned. 'Cullingoak way, I think it was.'

'Just one more question, Mrs Walsh.'

She looked at him, inured to official questions.

'This old man, Jenkins . . .'

'Yes?'

'Did he just have the one son?'

She shook her head. 'I did hear there was a daughter too but I never met her myself.'

*   *   *

The Rector and Mrs Meyton had taken Henrietta out to luncheon in Berebury after the inquest, Bill Thorpe had declined the invitation on the grounds that there were cows to be milked and other work to be done. It was Saturday afternoon, he explained awkwardly, and the men would have gone home. Whether this was so, or whether it was because of the silence which had followed his mention of marriage, nobody knew. He had made his apologies and gone before they left the Town Hall.

Arbican arranged for Henrietta to come to see him on Tuesday afternoon following the funeral in the morning. He had also enquired tactfully about her present finances.

There had been a lonely dignity about her reply, and Arbican had shaken hands all round and gone back to Calleford.

The mention of money, though, had provoked a memory on the Rector's part.

'This little matter of the medals,' he began over coffee.

'Yes,' she said politely. It wasn't a little matter but if Mr Meyton cared to put it like that . . .

'It solves one point which often puzzled me.' He took some sugar. 'Your mother . . .'

She wasn't her mother but Henrietta let that pass, too. She was beginning to be very tired now.

'Your mother was a very independent woman.'

'Yes.' That was absolutely true.

'Commendable, of course. Very. But not always the easiest sort of parishioner to help.'

'She didn't like being beholden to anyone.'

'Exactly.' He sipped his coffee. 'I well remember on one occasion I suggested that we approach the Calleshire Regimental Welfare Association . . .'

'Oh?'

'Yes. For a grant towards what is now, I believe, called "further education". In my day they called it . . .'

'After all,' put in Mrs Meyton kindly, 'that's what their funds are for, isn't it, dear?'

'Yes,' said Henrietta.

179

'But, of course,' went on Mrs Meyton, 'it was before you got the scholarship, and though they always thought you would get one, you can never be sure with scholarships, can you, dear?'

'Never,' said Henrietta fervently. She had never been certain herself, however often people had reassured her.

'Mrs Jenkins was quite sharp with me,' remembered the Rector ruefully. 'Polite, of course. She was always very polite, but firm. Scholarship or no scholarship she didn't want anything to do with it.'

Mrs Meyton said some people always did feel that way about grants.

The Rector set his cup down. 'But, of course, it all makes sense now we know that Cyril Jenkins wasn't killed in the war.'

'No, it doesn't,' said Henrietta.

'No?' The Rector looked mildly enquiring.

'You see,' said Henrietta, 'she told me that the Regimental Welfare people did help.'

'How very curious.'

'I know,' she said quickly, 'that the scholarship is the main thing but it's not really enough to—well—do more than manage.'

The Rector nodded. 'Quite so.'

'Money,' concluded Henrietta bleakly, 'came from somewhere for me when I got there.'

'You mean literally while you were there?'

'Yes. The Bursar saw that I had some at the

beginning of each term.' She flushed. 'I was told it was from the Calleshire Regiment, otherwise . . .'

'Otherwise,' interposed Mrs Meyton tactfully, 'I'm sure you wouldn't have wanted it any more than your mother would have done.'

'No.'

The Rector coughed. 'I think this may well be pertinent to Inspector Sloan's inquiry. Tell me, did the Bursar herself tell you where it came from?'

Henrietta frowned. 'Just that it was from the Regimental Welfare Association.'

'How very odd,' said the Rector of Larking.

*   *   *

This information was one more small piece which, when fitted exactly together with dozens of other small pieces of truth (and lies), detail, immutable fact, routine enquiry, known evidence, witnesses' stories and a detective's deductions, would, one day, produce a picture instead of a jigsaw.

This particular segment was relayed to Inspector Sloan when he made a routine telephone call to Berebury Police Station after leaving Rooden Parva. He and Crosby had called in at the Calleshire County Constabulary Headquarters to ascertain that the Calleford search for one Cyril Jenkins, wanted by the Berebury Division, had not yet

181

widened as far as the villages.

'Have a heart,' said Calleford's inspector on duty. He was an old friend of Sloan's called Blake. Rejecting—very vigorously—the obvious nickname of Sexton, he was known instead throughout the county as 'Digger'. 'There's dozens of small villages round here.'

Sloan nodded. 'Each with its own separate small register, I suppose?'

'That's right.' Blake pushed some tea in Sloan's direction. 'Your Superintendent as horrible as ever?'

'He doesn't change,' said Sloan.

'What with him and Happy Harry,' condoled Blake, 'I don't know how you manage, I really don't.'

For better or worse, Superintendent Leeyes was on duty for this weekend.

'Well, Sloan,' he barked down the telephone, 'how are you getting on?'

'Not too badly, sir. I've got a couple of promising lines of enquiry at the moment.'

'Hrrmph.' The Superintendent didn't like optimism in anyone, least of all in his subordinates. 'How promising?'

'Once upon a time, sir . . .'

'Is this a fairy story, Sloan?'

'A romance,' said Sloan shortly.

Leeyes grunted. 'Go on.'

'Once upon a time a certain Lady Garwell seems to have had an affair with a Major Hocklington.'

182

'Did she, bai Jove?' Mockingly.

'Yes, sir.'

'Got her name mentioned in the Mess?'

'I fear so, sir.'

'Things aren't what they were in my day, Sloan.'

'No, sir, except that this was all a long time ago.'

'That makes it worse,' retorted Leeyes promptly. 'Much worse. Morals were morals then. I don't know what they are now, I'm sure.'

'No, sir.' The Superintendent's views on vice were a byword in the Division.

'This Lady Garwell . . .'

'Yes, sir?'

'Are you trying to tell me that this girl who's the cause of all the trouble . . .'

That was a bit unfair. 'Henrietta, sir?' he said, putting as much injury into his tone as he dared.

'Henrietta.' He paused. 'Damn silly name for a girl, isn't it?'

'Old-fashioned,' said Sloan. 'Almost historical, you might say.'

Leeyes grunted. 'You think she's the—er—natural outcome of this affair?'

'I shouldn't like to say, sir. Not without further investigation. The General's practically gaga.'

'Doesn't mean a thing,' replied Leeyes swiftly. 'Or rather, it helps the case.'

'In what way, sir?'

Leeyes gave a chuckle that could only be described as salacious. 'Suppose he's married to some young thing . . .'

'Well?'

'Then she's much more likely to dilly-dally with this young Major Somebody or Other.'

'Hocklington, sir.'

'Much more likely,' repeated the Superintendent, who was by now getting to like the theory.

'Yes, sir, I see what you're driving at.' That was an understatement. 'But we don't know for certain that she was young.'

'Then we find out.'

'Yes, sir.' He swallowed. 'Any more than we know that Major Hocklington was young . . .'

'It stands to reason, Sloan, that they weren't old. Not if they had an affair.'

'No, sir.' Sloan didn't know Mrs Leeyes. Only that she was a little woman who bred cats. He wondered what it was like, being married to the Superintendent. He said inconsequentially, 'She's dead. Lady Garwell, I mean.'

'That doesn't stop her being Henrietta's mother,' snapped Leeyes.

'No, sir.'

'What about Major Hocklington?'

'Hirst—that's the General's man—didn't know.'

'Then find that out, Sloan, while you're

about it.'

'Yes, sir.'

'After all, she could have been in early middle age twenty-two years ago.' The Superintendent himself had been in early middle age for as long as Sloan could remember. 'And then died herself comparatively early.'

'Dead and never called her mother, in fact,' misquoted Sloan, who had once seen the Berebury Amateur Dramatic Society play *East Lynne*—and never forgotten the searing experience.

Literary allusions were lost upon the Superintendent who only said, 'And get Somerset House to turn up Hocklington-Garwell in the Births for twenty-one years ago. Or just plain Hocklington, if it comes to that.'

'Or Garwell,' pointed out Sloan. 'An illegitimate child takes the mother's surname, doesn't it?'

Leeyes grunted. 'At least it's not Smith. That's something to be thankful for.'

'You don't suppose,' asked Sloan hopefully, 'that her ladyship—if she was, in fact, Henrietta's mother—would have taken out an affiliation order against the father?'

'I do not,' said Leeyes.

'Pity.'

'Those sort of people don't.' An eager note crept into the Superintendent's voice. 'What they do, Sloan, is to dig up a faithful nanny who knows them well and they park the nanny and the infant in a cottage in the depths of the country.'

Sloan had been afraid of that.

'And,' Leeyes was warming to his theme, 'they support the child and the nanny from a distance.'

In Lady Garwell's case the distance—either way, so to speak—would be considerable, she being dead. Sloan presumed he meant Major Hocklington and said, 'Yes, sir, though I still can't see why Grace Jenkins should have to die just before the girl is twenty-one.'

'Ask Major Hocklington,' suggested Leeyes sepulchrally.

'Or, come to that, sir, why Grace Jenkins went to such enormous lengths to conceal the girl's true name and then talked quite happily about the Hocklington-Garwell's. If Lady Garwell were the mother, it doesn't make sense.'

'Someone has been sending the girl money at university,' said Leeyes. 'She and the clergyman have just been in to say so.'

'Maintenance,' said Sloan.

'Via the Bursar of her college.'

Sloan scribbled a note, his Sunday rest day vanishing into thin air. 'We could leave as soon as we've seen Cyril Jenkins . . .'

'And,' said Superintendent Leeyes nastily, 'you could see Cyril Jenkins as soon as you've had your tea and sympathy from Inspector

Blake.'

*   *   *

Cullingoak was more certainly a village than Rooden Parva. It had all the customary prerequisites thereof—a church standing foursquare in the middle, an old Manor House not very far away, shops, a post office, a row of almshouses down by the river, even a cricket ground.

'All we want,' observed Crosby, 'is a character called Jenkins.'

'No,' said Sloan, 'if the civil register is correct, he is called Cyril Edgar Jenkins and should live at number twelve High Street.'

'Dead easy,' Crosby swung the car round by the church. 'That'll be the road the post office is in, for sure.'

'Stop short,' Sloan told him. 'Just in case.'

'Sir, do you reckon he's her father?'

'I'll tell you that, Crosby, when I've seen him.'

'Likeness?'

'No.' Sloan remembered Mrs Walsh with a shudder. 'Something called eugenics.'

They found number twelve easily enough. Most of the High Street houses were old. They were small, too, but well cared for. Neither developers nor preservationists seemed to have got their hands on Cullingoak High Street. None of the houses were once 'wrong'

ones now 'done up' for 'right' people. There
was, too, a refreshing variety of coloured paint.
The door of number twelve was a deep green.
Sloan knocked on it.

There was no immediate reply.

'Just our luck,' said Crosby morosely, 'if he's
gone to a football match.'

It was implied—but not stated—that had
Detective Constable Crosby not had the
misfortune to be a member of Her Majesty's
Constabulary, that that was where he would
have been this Saturday afternoon in early
March.

'Berebury's playing Luston.'

'Really?'

'At home.'

That was the crowning injustice.

Next Saturday, Crosby would have to spend
good money travelling to Luston or Calleford
or Kinnisport to see some play.

Sloan knocked again.

There was no reply.

He looked up and down the street. There
would be a back way in somewhere. The two
policemen set off and walked until they found
it—a narrow, uneven way, leading to back
gates. Some as neatly painted as the front
doors. Some not. None numbered.

Crosby counted the houses back from the
beginning of the row. 'Nine, ten, eleven,
twelve.' He stopped at a gate that was still
hanging properly on both hinges. 'I reckon this

is the one, sir.'

'Well done,' said Sloan, who had already noticed that that back door was painted the same deep green as they had seen in the front. 'Perhaps he's one of those who'll answer the back door but not the front.'

They never discovered if this was so.

When they got to the back door it was ever so slightly ajar.

It opened a little further at Sloan's knock, and when there was no reply to this, Sloan opened it a bit more still and put his head round.

'Anyone at home?' he called out.

Cyril Jenkins was at home all right.

There was just one snag. He was dead.

Very.

CHAPTER FIFTEEN

Superintendent Leeyes was inclined to take the whole thing as a personal insult.

'Dead?' he shouted in affronted tones.

'Dead, sir.'

'He can't be . . .'

'He is.'

'Not our Jenkins,' he howled. 'Not the one we wanted. . .'

'Cyril Edgar,' said Sloan tersely. That much, at least, he had established before leaving number twelve and a pale but resolute Crosby standing guard. 'As for him being ours . . .'

'Yes?'

'I should think the fact that he's had his brains blown out rather clinches it.'

Sarcasm was a waste of time with the Superintendent.

'Self-inflicted?' he enquired eagerly.

'Impossible to say, sir, at this stage.'

'Was there a note?'

'No.' Sloan paused. 'Just a revolver.'

He wasn't sitting in the comfort of Inspector Blake's office now. He was in the cramped public telephone kiosk in Cullingoak High Street hoping that the young woman with a pram who was waiting to use it after him couldn't lip-read. At least she couldn't hear the Superintendent.

Sloan could.

'What sort of revolver?' he was asking.

'Service.' Sloan sighed. 'Old army issue.'

'Officers, for the use of, I suppose,' heavily.

'Yes, sir.'

Leeyes grunted. 'So it's still there?'

'Yes, sir. Silencer and all.'

'Not out of reach, I suppose?'

'No, sir.'

'I didn't think it would be.'

'By his right hand.'

'That's what I thought you were going to say. No hope of him being left-handed?'

'None. I checked.' Sloan had searched high and low for signs which would reveal whether Cyril Edgar Jenkins had taken his own life or if someone had taken it for him.

'I don't like it, Sloan.'

'No, sir.' Sloan didn't either. There was nothing to like in what he had just seen. The recently shot are seldom an attractive sight and Cyril Edgar Jenkins was no exception. He had been sitting down when it had happened and the result was indescribably messy. Experienced and hardened as he was, Sloan hadn't relished his quick examination. At least there hadn't been the additional burden of breaking the news to anyone. 'He lived alone,' he told Leeyes. 'Mrs Walsh out at Holly Tree Farm was quite right about his wife. She did die about eight years ago.'

'Who says so?'

'The woman next door. Remembers her well.'

'Which wife?' demanded Leeyes contentiously.

Sloan paused. 'The one he had been living with ever since he came to Cullingoak.'

'Ah, that's different.' Sloan could almost hear the Superintendent fumbling for the word he wanted. 'She might have just been his concubine.'

'Yes, sir, except that we couldn't find any record of a marriage between Cyril Edgar Jenkins and Grace Edith Wright in the first place . . .'

'I hadn't forgotten,' said Leeyes coldly. 'Now I suppose you're going to set about finding out if he was really married to this second woman . . .'

What Sloan wanted to do—and that very badly—was to set about finding out who had killed Cyril Jenkins.

'Yes, sir. In the meantime, do you think Dr Dabbe would come over?'

'I don't see why not,' said Leeyes largely. When he himself was working through a weekend he was usually in favour of as many people doing so as possible. 'What do you want him for?'

'Inspector Blake is handling the routine side of this, seeing as it's in his division,' said Sloan, 'but I want to talk to Dr Dabbe about blood.'

*　　*　　*

There was no shortage of this vital commodity in the living-room of number twelve Cullingoak High Street.

Sloan had vacated the telephone kiosk with a polite apology to the girl with the pram. In the manner of a generation brought up without courtesy, she had favoured him with a blank stare in return. Oddly disconcerted, but without time to wonder what things were coming to, he had hurried back to the house.

His friend Inspector Blake had just arrived

from Calleford and was standing surveying the scene.

'Nasty.'

Sloan could only agree. Crosby, who had been surveying the same scene for rather longer and more consistently than either Blake or Sloan, was looking rather green at the gills.

'He got wind that you wanted a little chat, did he then?' asked Digger Blake. He had brought his own photographer and finger-print man with him and he motioned them now to go ahead with their gruesome work.

'Perhaps,' said Sloan slowly. 'Perhaps not.'

'Not a coincidence anyway,' said Blake.

'No. Someone knew.'

'Many people realise you wanted this word or two with him?' Digger's questions were usually obliquely phrased.

'Enough.' Sloan took a deep breath. 'A girl who said she saw him in Calleford yesterday afternoon.' Henrietta had probably been right about that, now he came to think of it, but how significant it was he couldn't sort out. Not for the moment. 'Her solicitor. He knew, of course. He's called Arbican.'

'That'll be Waind, Arbican and Waind, in Ox Lane,' said Blake. 'There's only him left in the firm now.'

'And a young man called Bill Thorpe . . .' He hesitated. 'I can't make up my mind about him.'

'What's his trouble?'

193

'Too ardent for my liking.'

'It's not whether *you* like it, old chap,' grinned Blake. 'It's if the lady likes it.'

'She's got quite enough on her plate as it is,' said Sloan primly.

And he told Digger the whole story.

'A proper mix-up, isn't it?' Blake said appreciatively. 'Rather you than me.'

'Thank you, Crosby, if you want to be sick go outside.'

'Who else knew you wanted Jenkins?' asked Blake, who was nowhere near as casual as he sounded.

Sloan frowned. 'The Rector of Larking and his wife. Meyton's their name.'

'Lesson One,' quoted Blake. 'The cloth isn't always what it . . .'

'It is this time.'

'Oh, really? And who else is in the know?'

'No one that I know of. There's a James Heber Hibbs, Esquire . . .'

'Gent?'

'Landed gent,' said Sloan firmly, 'of The Hall, Larking, but he doesn't know about Jenkins. Not unless the girl's told him and I don't quite see when she would have done. Owns about half the village if you ask me.'

'For Hibbs read Nibs,' said Digger frivolously. 'Has he got a missus?'

'Yes, but you call her madam, my lad.'

'And their connection with this case?'

'Obscure,' said Sloan bitterly.

194

'Anyone else?'

Sloan hesitated. 'There's a certain Major Hocklington, but . . .'

'But what?'

'He might be dead.'

'I see. Well, when you've made your mind up . . .'

'He might have had the MC and the DSO, too.'

'That'll be a great help in finding him,' murmured Digger affably, 'but I'd rather he had a scar on his left cheek, if it's all the same to you.'

'There's always the possibility,' said Sloan, 'that Major Hocklington had someone acting for him.'

'If he's dead, for instance?' Blake moved out of the photographer's line of vision.

'That's right.'

Blake pointed the same way as the photographer's camera. '*He's* not going to tell you. Not now.'

'No,' said Sloan morbidly, 'though, oddly enough, I'm after his blood too.'

*   *   *

It was something after eight o'clock that evening when Inspector Sloan, supported by a still rather wan-looking Constable Crosby, reported back to Superintendent Leeyes in person at the Berebury Police Station.

'As pretty a kettle of fish, sir,' Sloan said, 'as you'll find anywhere.'

'Suicide or murder?' demanded Leeyes.

But it wasn't as simple as that.

Dr Dabbe had got to Cullingoak at a speed which, as far as Sloan was concerned, didn't bear thinking about. He was well known as the fastest driver in Calleshire and nothing that his arch enemy, Inspector Harpe of Traffic Division, could do seemed to slow him down at all.

At the house Dr Dabbe had met his opposite number, the Consultant Pathologist for East Calleshire, Dr Sorley McPherson. The two doctors had treated each other with an elaborate and ritual courtesy which reminded Sloan of nothing so much as the courtship display of a pair of ducks at mating time.

With professional punctiliousness each had invited the other's opinion on every possible point.

The upshot—after, in Sloan's private opinion, a great deal of unnecessasry billing and cooing—was that Cyril Edgar Jenkins had probably been shot in the head by someone sitting opposite him across the table, who had pulled out a revolver and leaned forward.

'We can't be certain, of courrrse,' Dr Sorley McPherson had rolled his 'r's' in an intimidating way, 'but it looks as if the rrevolver was placed in deceased's rright hand after death.'

'I see, doctor.'

'Suicide,' he went on, 'was doubtless meant to be inferrrred.'

Sloan thought the 'r's' were never going to stop.

'We'll be needing a wee look at the poor chap's fingerprints on the revolver handle. D'you not agree, Dabbe?'

Dr Dabbe had agreed. The powder burns, the position of the shot, the body, the revolver, all indicated murder made to look like suicide.

Sloan said all this to the Superintendent. 'But only inferred, sir. Not proved yet.'

Leeyes snorted in a dissatisfied way. 'Except, then, that he's dead, we're no further forward.'

Sloan said nothing. If Leeyes cared to regard that as progress there was nothing he could say.

'What about the blood?' said the Superintendent.

'Dr Dabbe's grouping it now. He's going to ring.'

Leeyes drummed a pencil on his desk. 'You say no one in Cullingoak saw or heard anything?'

'No one. The people in the house next door on one side were out and the woman in the other always has a lay-down after her lunch. Anyone could walk in the back, just like we did. He did have a job in Calleford, by the way. She confirms that.'

'No other children?'

'No, sir, not that she knew of.'

Leeyes grunted. 'And Major Hocklington—where have you got with him?'

'The Army are doing what they can, but . . .'

'I know, Sloan. Saturday night's not the best time.'

'No, sir. If he were a serving officer now it would be quite simple.'

'I presume,' coldly, 'you checked the Army List days ago.'

'Yes, sir.'

'So we have to wait.' Leeyes wasn't good at waiting.

'Yes, sir.'

'And our other friends?'

Sloan turned back the pages of his notebook though he knew well enough what was written there. 'Bill Thorpe excused himself pretty smartly after the inquest and went off just before Arbican went back to Calleford.'

'Went off where?'

'Larking, he says. He wouldn't have lunch in Berebury with the Meytons and Henrietta.'

'Why not?'

'Said he hadn't time. Had to get back to the farm.'

'And did he?'

Sloan said carefully, 'No one happened to see him at Shire Oak—which, of course, is not to say he wasn't there.'

'Did you get his background?'

'It seems all right, sir. Second son of middling size farmer with quite a good name locally. Lived in Larking all his life. Known Henrietta ever since she was a child. Been home from Agricultural College for about two years.'

'Found the body, could have knocked it down, stuck to the girl like a leech since it happened, wants to marry her quickly.' Leeyes's rasping tones supplanted Sloan's matter-of-fact report. 'Could have killed Cyril Jenkins. Could have known the whole story. Could have wanted money . . .'

'Why, sir?'

'He's the second son, Sloan. You've just said so.'

'Yes, sir.' It was futile to argue with the Superintendent.

Leeyes grunted. 'And this other fellow—the one with the money. What about him?'

'Hibbs?' said Sloan. The Superintendent was always suspicious of people with money, assuming it, in the absence of specific evidence to the contrary, to be ill-gotten. Sloan cleared his throat uneasily. 'He and his wife went into Calleford for the day.'

'They did what?'

'Went into Calleford,' repeated Sloan, going on hastily, 'they had a meal at "The Tabard". She went to a dress shop and he called in at a corn chandler's in the morning . . .'

'Whatever for?'

199

'He's hand-rearing some pheasants this year, sir.' Sloan himself had always wondered what you did at a corn chandler's. 'And he visited a wine merchant's just after lunch.'

'When was Jenkins shot?'

'Roughly about three o'clock.' The two pathologists had been as agreed on this as on everything else.

'Could he have done it?'

'Easily. So could Bill Thorpe. Anyone could have done it. Even Arbican if he had had a mind to—to say nothing of Major Hocklington. Always supposing he exists.'

Leeyes was thinking, not listening. 'Sounds as if it could have been someone Jenkins knew fairly well—all this business of back doors and sitting down at the table together.'

'Yes, sir.' Inspector Blake had cottoned on to that fact, too, as he went methodically about his routine investigation. 'The only trouble is that we don't know who it was that Cyril Jenkins knew.'

'No.' Leeyes frowned. 'Or what.'

'The whole story, I expect,' said Sloan gloomily. 'That's why he had to go.'

The telephone rang. Leeyes answered it and handed it to Sloan. 'The hospital,' he said. 'Dr Dabbe.'

Sloan listened for a moment, thanked the pathologist, promised to let him know something later and then rang off.

'The late Cyril Jenkins's blood was group

AB,' he announced.

'And the girl's?' asked Leeyes.

'We don't know yet. We're going to ask her if we can have some to see.'

'Tricky,' pronounced Leeyes. 'Be very careful . . .'

'Why, sir?'

'Because if this case ever gets to court,' he stressed the word 'if' heavily, and implied if it didn't it wouldn't be Sloan's fault, 'if it does then you will probably find some clever young man arguing that you've committed a technical assault, that's why.'

'But if the putative father . . .'

'Get as many witnesses to her free consent as you can,' advised Leeyes sourly. 'That's all.'

'Yes, sir,' promised Sloan, 'and then we're going to Camford to see the Bursar of her college.'

He and Crosby got up to go but Sloan turned short of the door.

'That AB blood group, sir . . .'

'What about it?'

'It's the same as Grace Jenkins's.'

'Well?'

'If the girl hadn't said the woman's maiden name was Wright, I could make out quite a good case for Grace Jenkins and Cyril Jenkins being brother and sister.'

CHAPTER SIXTEEN

'Dead?' said Henrietta dully.

'I'm afraid so.' Sloan wished her reaction could have been more like the Superintendent's. It couldn't be doing her any good sitting here in Boundary Cottage, hanging on to her self-control with an effort that was painful to watch.

'Inspector,' she whispered. 'I killed him, didn't I?'

'I don't think so, miss,' responded Sloan, surprised.

'I don't mean actually.' She twisted her hands together in her lap. 'But as good as . . .'

'I don't see quite how, miss, if you'll forgive my saying so.' It occurred to Sloan for the first time that this was what people meant by wringing their hands.

'By seeing him.' She swallowed. 'Don't you understand? If I hadn't seen him yesterday and recognised him, then he wouldn't be dead today.'

This, thought Sloan, might well be true.

'Perhaps, miss,' he said quietly, 'but that doesn't make it your fault.'

'I haven't got the Evil Eye, or anything like that, I know, but,' she sounded utterly shaken, 'but if he was my father and I've been the means of killing him . . . I don't think I could

202

bear that.'

Sloan coughed. She had given him the opening he wanted. 'That's one of the reasons why we've come, miss. About the question of this Cyril Jenkins being your father.'

'Do you know then?' directly.

'No, miss. We don't think he was but we can't prove it either way . . . yet.'

'Yet?' she asked quickly.

'Dr Dabbe—he's the hospital pathologist, miss—he says a blood test can prove something but not everything.'

'Anything,' she said fervently, 'would be better than this not knowing.'

'If you agreed to it,' he said carefully, 'and I must make it clear you don't have to, it might just prove Cyril Jenkins wasn't your father and never could have been.'

'Then,' said Henrietta in a perplexed way, 'who was he and what had he got to do with us?'

'We don't know.'

'Just that he's dead.'

'That's right, miss.'

She looked at him. 'How soon can you do this blood thing?'

'If you would come with me to the telephone and ring Mr Arbican—he's entitled to advise you against it, if he thinks fit—then I could ring Dr Dabbe now.' He grinned. 'It won't take him long to get here.'

It didn't.

A stranger would have noticed nothing out of the ordinary should he have chanced to visit the village of Larking the next morning. Not, of course, that there were any strangers there. Larking was not that sort of village. A Sunday calm had descended upon the place and the inhabitants were going about their usual avocations. About a quarter of them were in church. At Matins.

Henrietta was there.

She was staying at the Rectory now. She had been in that pleasant house on the green since late last night. Just before he had left, Inspector Sloan had said he would be greatly obliged if Miss Jenkins would take herself to the Rectory for the night.

'Otherwise, miss,' he had gone on, 'I shall have to spare a man to stay here and keep an eye on you.'

Mrs Meyton, bless her, had been only too happy to have her under the Rectory wing and Henrietta had been popped between clean sheets in the spare bed without fuss or botheration. The Rector presumably had been wrestling with his sermon because she hadn't seen him at all last night nor this morning when he had breakfasted alone between early service and Matins.

James Heber Hibbs read the First Lesson.

Henrietta was devoutly thankful that today was one of the Sundays in Lent, which meant that she didn't have to listen while he fought his way through the genealogical tree of Abraham who begat Isaac who begat Jacob who begat . . .

She could listen to the Book of Numbers (Chapter 14, verse 26) with equanimity but she didn't think she could bear to hear that unconscionable list of who begat whom when she was still no nearer knowing the father who had begat her. She sat, hands folded in front of her, while James Hibbs's neat unaccented voice retailed what the Lord spake unto Moses and unto Aaron.

She felt curiously detached. No doubt the events of the past week would fade into proportion in time just as those of the Old Testament had done but at the moment she wasn't sure.

'. . . save Caleb the son of Jephunneh, and Joshua, the son of Nun,' said James Hibbs in those English upper-middle-class tones considered suitable for readings in church which would have greatly surprised both Caleb and Joshua, son of Nun, had they heard them.

That had been how a man was known in those far-off days, of course. It mattered very much whose son you were, which tribe you belonged to . . . One day, perhaps, she, Henrietta, would be able once again to look into a mirror without wondering who it was she saw there, but not yet . . . definitely not yet.

A fragment of an almost forgotten newspaper article came back to her while she was sitting quietly in the pew. Somewhere she had read once that to undermine the resistance of prisoners in a concentration camp their captors first took away every single thing the poor unfortunates could call their own—papers, watches, rings, glasses, false teeth even. It was the first step towards the deliberate destruction of personality. After that the prisoners, utterly demoralised, began to doubt their very identity. Lacking reassurance in the matter, then surely existence itself would seem pointless, resistance became more meaningless still.

'. . . Here endeth the First Lesson,' declared James Hibbs, leaving the lectern and going back to his wife in the pew which, abolition of pew rents or not, inalienably belonged to The Hall. He still walked like a soldier.

It didn't seem possible that last Sunday Henrietta had been at university in Camford, Finals the biggest landmark in her immediate future, Bill Thorpe more nebulously beyond . . . her mother always in the background.

Only she wasn't her mother.

And the background had changed as suddenly as a theatre back-cloth. The man in the photograph on the mantelpiece had come briefly alive—and mysteriously was now dead again.

Uncomforted by the Rector's blessing at the end of the service, she waited in her seat until the church emptied. That, at least, saved her from all but the most barefaced of the curious. Mrs Meyton insisted upon her lunching at the Rectory. Henrietta demurred.

'When, my dear child, have you had time to buy food?' Mrs Meyton asked.

Henrietta spoke vaguely of some cheese but was overruled by an indignant Mrs Meyton.

'Certainly not,' said that lady roundly.

It wasn't the happiest of meals. Henrietta ate her way through roast beef and Yorkshire pudding without appetite, one thing uppermost in her mind.

'They don't say very much in the newspapers,' she murmured. 'And the Inspector didn't tell me anything. Just that he was found dead . . .'

This was only partly true. The Sunday newspapers not available at the Rectory had covered the death of Cyril Jenkins fairly graphically ('Widower Dies', 'Gunshot Death', 'Bloodstained Room') but neither the Meytons nor Henrietta knew this.

The Rector nodded. 'I fear there is little doubt that his death is significant.'

'What I want to know,' demanded Henrietta almost angrily, 'is if he was my father or not.'

She didn't know yet if the little red bottle borne away last night by the pathologist—after a few mild, stock jokes about vampires—was going to tell her that or not.

Mr Meyton nodded again. 'Quite so.'

And in an anguished whisper, 'And who killed him.'

'My dear,' began Mrs Meyton, 'should you concern yourself with . . .'

'Yes,' intervened the Rector firmly, 'she should.'

'I must know,' said Henrietta firmly, a tremulous note coming into her voice in spite of all her efforts to suppress it, 'whether I am misbegotten or not.'

*   *   *

Dr Dabbe could have told her something.

He telephoned the Berebury Police Station.

'That you, Sloan? I've done a grouping.'

'Yes, doctor?'

'The girl's group O.'

Sloan wrote it down. 'Jenkins was AB, wasn't he?'

'That's right.'

'That means, doctor, that . . .'

'That he is not the girl's father,' said Dr Dabbe dogmatically. 'And that's conclusive and irrespective of the mother's blood group. A man who's AB blood group cannot have a child belonging to O blood group.'

'Thank you, doctor. Thank you very much. That's a great help . . .'

'It's an indisputable fact,' said Dr Dabbe

tartly, 'which is more to the point.'

Inspector Sloan and Constable Crosby reached the university town of Camford just before noon on the Sunday morning and drove straight to the centre of that many-tower'd Camelot. A friendly colleague directed them to Boleyn College.

'Funny person to call a ladies' college after,' muttered Constable Crosby, putting the car into gear again. 'Wasn't she one of Henry the Eighth's . . .'

'Yes,' said Sloan shortly, 'she was.'

They found the decorous brick building on the outskirts of the town and waited while the porter set about finding the Bursar, Miss Wotherspoon. She did not keep them long. A petite bird-like figure came tripping down the corridor. Sloan explained that he had come about Henrietta Jenkins.

'Jenkins?' said Miss Wotherspoon. 'Nice girl.'

'Yes.'

'Not a First . . .'

'Oh?' said Sloan, who hadn't the faintest idea what she was talking about but wasn't prepared to say so.

'Perhaps a Second but I shouldn't count on it.'

'No . . .'

'And,' Miss Wotherspoon sighed, 'there'll be some young man waiting to marry her who doesn't care either way.'

'There is.'

Miss Wotherspoon shook her head. 'No use trying to stop them,' she said briskly. 'Take my advice about that. They hold it against you for ever afterwards.'

On that point Sloan was agreed with the Bursar, but before he could say anything further she went on, 'But I've just remembered, Henrietta Jenkins hasn't got a father.'

'No,' agreed Sloan. This, he thought, was true. If by any chance Cyril Jenkins had been her father, he wasn't alive any more to tell the tale.

'Then you must be . . .' began Miss Wotherspoon—and stopped.

'Who?' prompted Sloan gently.

But he wasn't catching the Bursar out that way.

'No,' she said. 'I think you must tell me.'

'The police,' admitted Sloan regretfully.

'You had better come to my study.'

She listened to Sloan's tale without interruption, waited until he was quite finished and then announced that she would have to take him to the Principal. He and Crosby tramped off after her and soon found themselves in a very gracious room indeed.

The Principal was an impressive woman by any standard save that of fashion. She had a calm, still authority, responsive yet unsurprised. Sloan and Crosby were invited to

210

settle into chintz armchairs and to repeat their story.

'I see,' said the Principal when he had done—and not before. Both women exhibited a rare facility for listening. If this was the result of the education of women, then Sloan—for one—was all in favour.

'You will be able to see our difficulty, too,' said Sloan. 'You have this girl whom we have reason to believe is being maintained here beyond such scholarships and grants as she may have been awarded.'

'True,' said the Bursar, 'but we were given funds on the condition that she never knew the source.'

'I don't think she need,' replied Sloan seriously. 'I can't give you any sort of undertaking because this is a criminal case but unless such facts came out in open court I see no reason myself why she should be told.'

'In that case,' pronounced the Principal, 'I see no reason why Miss Wotherspoon should not divulge the—er—donor's name to you.'

'Thank you, madam.'

Miss Wotherspoon disappeared in the direction of her study and returned waving a piece of paper.

'It wasn't a lot,' she said. 'Just a small cheque each term to make things more . . . what is the word I'm looking for?'

The word Sloan was looking for—and that very badly—was on the paper the Bursar was holding. He retained his selfcontrol with difficulty.

'Tolerable,' decided Miss Wotherspoon brightly. 'Grants and scholarships are all very well but a girl needs a bit more than that if she's going to get the most out of Camford.'

'The name,' pleaded Sloan.

Miss Wotherspoon looked at the paper in her hand. 'Would it,' she said rather doubtfully, 'be Hibbs? That's what it looks like to me. J. A. H. Hibbs.'

Sloan groaned aloud.

'The Hall, Larking, Calleshire,' said Miss Wotherspoon for good measure.

'He never said why, I suppose?' asked Sloan.

'Just a brief note with the first cheque saying he thought funds at home were rather low and the enclosed might help.' Miss Wotherspoon waved a hand vaguely. 'That sort of thing. The only condition was that the girl didn't know. I could tell her what I liked.'

'And what did you tell her?'

'A Service charity,' said the Bursar promptly. 'Plenty of girls receive money from them. There was no reason why she shouldn't.'

'There was,' said the Principal unexpectedly.

Sloan, Crosby and Miss Wotherspoon all turned in her direction.

'A very good reason,' said the Principal.

Sloan cleared his throat. It had suddenly seemed to go very dry.

'What was that, madam?' She looked the sort of person who could tell a good reason from a bad one. If she thought it a very good reason . . .

'She wasn't who she thought she was.'

'No. We have established that, madam, in Calleshire, but I should dearly like to know how you . . .'

'For entry to Boleyn College, Inspector, we require a sight of the candidate's birth certificate . . .'

'Of course!' Sloan brought his hand down on the arm of the chintz-covered chair with a mighty slap. 'We should have thought of that before.'

'Not, you understand, in order to confirm family details. We are not concerned,' here academic scruple raised its head, 'with the father's occupation but with the age of the candidate.'

'Quite so,' said Sloan, who was concerned about something quite different still. 'How very stupid we have been, madam. This would have saved us a great deal—might even have saved a life.'

As before, the Principal waited until he was quite finished before she continued. 'Naturally, this also applied in the case of Henrietta Jenkins.'

'Yes . . .' eagerly.

'With her birth certificate came a letter from the woman she believed to be her mother

'...,'

'Grace Jenkins . . .'

The Principal inclined her head. 'This letter, which was addressed to me personally, explained that the girl did not know the name of her real parents and was not to be told it until she was twenty-one.'

'Yes?' even more eagerly.

'This I felt was a most unwise procedure and one I would have counselled against most strongly. However . . .'

Sloan was sitting on the very edge of his chair. 'Yes?'

'However, her—er—guardian . . . is that who she was?'

'In a way,' said Sloan grimly.

'Her guardian's wishes were entitled to be respected.'

'And?'

'The birth certificate was returned to Mrs Jenkins and I have not mentioned the fact to anyone until today.'

'The name,' said Sloan. 'What was the name?'

The Principal paused. 'I don't think I can be absolutely certain . . .'

'Henrietta who?' said Sloan urgently.

'I am left with the impression that it was Mantriot.'

*   *   *

214

Bill Thorpe walked down from Shire Oak Farm about half-past two and called for Henrietta at the Rectory. She went with him as much because the Meytons were obviously used to a post-prandial snooze on Sunday afternoons, as for any other reason.

'I told you I'd seen Cyril Jenkins yesterday,' she said by way of greeting. Her feelings towards Bill Thorpe were decidedly ambivalent.

'You did,' agreed Thorpe.

'What price him being my father?'

'Perhaps.' Diplomatically.

'Or do you still think it doesn't matter?'

Bill Thorpe grinned. 'A gooseberry bush would still do for me.'

'Well!' exploded Henrietta crossly, 'I think you're the . . .'

'Or a carpet bag. At Victoria Station.' He took a couple of paces back and raised an arm to ward off an imaginary blow. 'The Brighton line, of course.'

'The police,' said Henrietta, ignoring this, 'probably won't believe me, but . . .'

'The police,' declared Bill, 'are trained not to believe anybody. It is the secret of their success.'

They had passed the entrance gates to The Hall now and were walking down the road to Boundary Cottage.

'I've just thought of something,' said Henrietta suddenly.

'What's that?'

'If I'm not who I thought I was . . .'

'Yes?'

'I don't have to be an only child.'

'No,' agreed Bill Thorpe.

'I thought you were going to say that didn't matter either,' she said, a little deflated.

'But it does.' Bill Thorpe pushed open the gate of Boundary Cottage and stood back to let her go first. 'Very much.'

'Very much?'

'Just in the one set of circumstances.' He turned to shut the gate behind him, farmer through and through. 'Unlikely, I know, but . . .'

'But what?'

'We must make absolutely sure,' he said gravely, 'that you and I are not brother and sister. I have every intention of marrying you and that's the only thing which could stop me.'

She laughed at last. 'Not allowed outside ancient Egypt?'

'The word, I believe, is taboo.'

Henrietta led the way up to the front door, still laughing. She stopped as soon as she opened it.

'Whatever's the matter?' enquired Bill quickly. 'You've gone quite white.'

She stood stock-still on the door-step.

'Someone's been in here,' she said, 'since I left last night.'

CHAPTER SEVENTEEN

There was no question of either of them having a meal. It was offered by the Principal of Boleyn College and seconded by the Bursar. Even in the ordinary way Inspector Sloan (if not Detective Constable Crosby) would have refused an invitation to sit down with three hundred young ladies of academic bent. Today was not ordinary. Their one aim was to get back to Calleshire with all possible speed. They hurried away from the dreaming spires without so much as a backward glance and got out on the open road.

'Hibbs,' said Crosby glumly.

'Mantriot,' countered Sloan.

Crosby executed a driving manoeuvre between two lorries and an articulated trailer which he had not learnt at the police motoring school.

'It isn't going to help our investigations, Constable,' said Sloan testily, 'if we none of us live to find out about Mantriot.'

'No, sir,' Crosby lifted his foot off the accelerator a fraction. 'I think I know something already.'

'You what?'

'The name, sir, it rings a bell.'

'In what way?'

'I don't know.

'Then think.'

'Yes, sir.'

There was a short silence in the police car while Constable Crosby thought. This did not preclude him overtaking a sports car at a speed Sloan did not relish.

'If,' said Sloan, 'you would think any better away from the wheel, I will take it.'

'That's all right, sir, thank you. I don't have to think about my driving.'

'I noticed,' said Sloan sweetly.

There was another silence while they ate up the miles at a speed which was specifically forbidden at the police motoring school.

Crosby was observed to be frowning.

'Well?' said Sloan hopefully.

'It's in the past somewhere, sir.'

'I know that.'

'I mean what I remember.'

Sloan did not attempt to sort this out. He was now too busy wishing he had led a better life—time for reform having obviously run out.

The car swerved dangerously. 'I've got it, sir.'

'Have you?' muttered Sloan between clenched teeth. 'Then slow down.' He started to breathe again as the fields stopped flashing by quite so quickly. 'Now tell me.'

'I can't tell you anything, sir,' said Crosby helpfully, 'except that I remember the name.'

'Where?'

'The past.'

'I wish,' said Sloan, made irritable by fear, 'that you would stop saying that.'

'I mean, sir,' Crosby was never good at explanations, 'when I was trying to learn about the past.'

'Light is beginning to dawn, Crosby. Go on.'

'It all started when I didn't know who George Smith was, sir.'

'I'm not sure that I do either.'

'He drowned his wives,' said Crosby reproachfully. 'All of them.'

'Oh, him.'

'Yes, sir, but I didn't know at the time and they pulled my leg a bit at the station.'

'I'll bet they did.'

'Every time anyone mentioned the word "bath". So Sergeant Gelven—he said if I was ever going to get anywhere, I'd better read up famous cases.'

'The Tichborne Claimant,' remembered Sloan suddenly. 'That's how you knew about that . . .'

'Yes, sir.'

'But,' puzzled, 'how does Mantriot come in?'

'It's not a Famous Case, sir, I do know that.'

'Not yet it isn't,' retorted Sloan, 'but I shouldn't count on it staying that way.'

'So it must be a local one. After I'd done the others, sir, I went back through the Calleshire records. That's where I've seen the name, I'm sure.' Crosby spotted a rival county's radar trap and slowed down. 'But I don't remember when or where.'

'We'll soon find out,' said Sloan pleasantly. 'You can go through them again until you find it.'

*   *   *

Superintendent Leeyes's afternoon cups of tea were rather like American television shows which went from the late show to the late, late show to the late, late, late show thence merging imperceptibly into the early, early, early show, the early, early show and naturally enough the early show. His tea went on the same principle—the after lunch cup, the early afternoon cup, the middle of the afternoon one and so forth. It was impossible for Sloan and Crosby to guess which one he was at when they arrived back in Berebury.

'We've got him,' announced Leeyes triumphantly.

Sloan shook his head. 'I should say that gift lets Hibbs out.'

'And I should say,' retorted Leeyes robustly, 'that it lets him in.'

'I'll go down there at once, sir, and see.'

'There's one other thing, Sloan . . .'

'Sir?'

'This girl—I think she's starting to imagine things now . . .'

'I should very much doubt that.'

220

'You sent her away from home last night.'

'I tried to. I don't know if she went but I told PC Hepple he was to keep an eye on her if she didn't.'

'She did. To the Rectory. But she and the Thorpe boy went back to Boundary Cottage after lunch.'

'Yes?' said Sloan alertly.

'He rang up about an hour ago to say the girl swears someone's been in the cottage overnight.'

Sloan expired audibly. 'I thought they might. That's why . . .'

'Someone's got a key,' snapped Leeyes. 'We've known that all along. Why didn't you have the lock changed?'

'I wanted them to show their hand,' said Sloan simply. 'And they have.'

*   *   *

Sunday was Sunday as far as James Hibbs and his wife were concerned. It was late afternoon when Sloan and Crosby arrived at The Hall. This time, being Sunday, they were shown into the drawing-room. Tea at The Hall on Sundays would always be in the drawing-room. Tea this afternoon had been eaten but not cleared away. A beautiful Georgian silver teapot graced the tea-tray, some sandwiches and a jar of Gentlemen's Relish stood beside it. Sloan hankered after the sandwiches but

221

not the tea. He had had some tea from a tea-pot like that once before—pale, straw-coloured stuff with a sinister taste. He had not been at all surprised to learn that it had come from China.

The two policemen were invited to sit on the large sofa in front of the fire. Their combined weights sank into it. Constable Crosby was the heavier of the two which gave Sloan's sitting position an odd list to starboard. No one could have described it as an advantageous situation from which to conduct an interview in what Sloan now knew to be a double murder case.

His tone was sharper that it had been earlier.

'You said before, sir, that you had never seen Mrs Grace Jenkins until she came to Larking.'

'Actually,' said Hibbs mildly, 'I don't think I saw her until quite a while afterwards. I was away myself, you know, at the time. I told you, if you remember, my old agent fixed up the tenancy.'

'Yes, sir, you did. You showed me a letter.'

'Ah, yes.'

'You showed me a letter,' said Sloan accusingly, 'but I don't think you told me the whole story.'

'No, Inspector? What else was it you wanted to know?'

'Why you sent money to be given to

222

Henrietta at the university?' Sloan asked the question of James Hibbs but he was looking at Mrs Hibbs's face while he spoke.

It did not change.

'Come, now,' Hibbs smiled disarmingly. 'You surely can't expect me to have told you a thing like that.'

Mrs Hibbs nodded in agreement with her husband and said in her pleasant deep voice: 'It was a private benefaction, Inspector. Nothing to do with anyone but ourselves.'

'At the moment, madam, everything to do with Henrietta is to do with us.'

'We could see a need,' said Hibbs, embarrassed, 'that's all.'

'So you set about filling it?'

'That's right, Inspector. I don't hold with all these national appeals. I'd rather give on my own.'

'Charity beginning at home, sir?'

Hibbs flushed. 'If you care to put it like that.'

'I see, sir.' Sloan started to heave himself out of the sofa. 'I asked you earlier if the name Hocklington-Garwell conveyed anything to you and you said no.'

'I did.'

'I'm asking you now if you have ever heard the name of Mantriot before.'

'Hugo, you mean?'

'Perhaps. Or Michael. Michael was killed early on. Dunkirk.'

James Hibbs said very soberly. 'Yes, Inspector, of course I have . . .'

'Of course?'

'He was in the East Callies and I was in the West but . . . Good Lord . . . I never thought!'

'You never thought what, sir?'

'Of Henrietta being Hugo's.' Hibbs frowned into the distance. 'I must say, Inspector, in all the years I've been here it's never crossed my mind for an instant.'

'What hasn't, sir?'

'Inspector, are you trying to tell us that Henrietta Jenkins is the Mantriot baby?'

'I don't know, sir. Suppose you tell me.'

'You won't remember, of course . . .'

'No, sir.'

'It was all pretty ghastly,' said Hibbs. 'It was in the war, you know. Towards the end. Hugo had had a bad war one way and another . . .'

That, thought Sloan with mounting excitement, would explain the DSO and the MC.

'. . . but he got home for a spot of leave just after the baby was born. Everyone was delighted, naturally, but something went very wrong.'

'What?'

'I don't know.' Hibbs shrugged his well-tailored shoulders. 'They said afterwards that his mind must have turned. Common enough thing to happen at the time, of course. He must have been through some rotten experiences before the end. Could have happened to any of us, I suppose.'

'What could, sir?' very quietly.

'Didn't you know, Inspector?'

'No, sir. Not yet.'

'One day he killed his wife and then he shot himself.' Hibbs shook his head sadly. 'It's all a long time ago now, of course. Some nanny took the baby . . .'

'Grace Jenkins!' cried Mrs Hibbs suddenly.

'Bless my soul,' said Hibbs.

Sloan started to move towards the door when Hibbs burst out laughing.

'It's a funny world, Inspector. Here's my wife and I sending to Eleanor Leslie's daughter . . .'

'What's so odd about that, sir?'

Hibbs stopped laughing and said solemnly. 'Because Eleanor Leslie—that's who Hugo Mantriot married—was a great deal wealthier than you or I shall ever be. She was old Bruce Leslie's only daughter. You know—the shipping people.'

CHAPTER EIGHTEEN

The next two hours were the busiest young Constable Crosby had ever known. First of all he was put down in front of a pile of dusty old records and told to get on with it. This was particularly difficult as Superintendent Leeyes and Detective Inspector Sloan were talking round him.

'So Hibbs realised you'd got onto the name and decided to play the surprised innocent,' said Leeyes trenchantly.

'I'm not sure, sir. If so, he did it very well . . .'

'He would,' snapped Leeyes. 'He's had plenty of time to get ready for it. Twenty-one years.'

'The important thing, of course,' said Sloan, 'is obviously the girl's twenty-first birthday. That'll be the day when she'll come into her mother's money for sure.'

'I should like to be quite certain that the young man at the farm didn't know that,' said Leeyes. 'His—er—wooing was a bit brisk.'

'But not until after Grace Jenkins died,' pointed out Sloan. 'He'd agreed to stay in the background until Henrietta finished at Boleyn College.'

'Then,' said Leeyes pouncing, 'he kills Grace Jenkins and goes ahead with Henrietta.'

Sloan shook his head. 'What I would like to know, sir, is where Cyril Jenkins comes in.'

'I think he committed just the one mistake,' said Leeyes shrewdly. 'He knew who Henrietta was and he was probably the last person alive who did.'

'Bar one,' said Sloan ominously.

'Bar one,' agreed Leeyes. 'And what do you propose to do about it, Sloan?'

226

'Set a trap,' said that policeman, 'so deep that there'll be no getting out of it.'

* * *

It was half an hour later when Crosby gave a loud cry.

'Found something interesting, Constable?'

'A report of a road accident, sir.'

'When?'

Crosby glanced up to the top of the newspaper page. 'Almost six months ago.'

Sloan stepped over and read it.

'Do you believe in coincidence, Crosby?'

'No, sir.'

'Neither do I.'

'There's something I do believe in, sir.'

'What's that?'

'Practice making perfect.'

'You can say that again,' said Sloan warmly, 'we've just found this.'

Crosby read out the faded cutting which Inspector Sloan handed him. 'This bit, sir? "Deceased had apparently shot himself whilst sitting down. The weapon had fallen on to the table in front of him . . ."' Crosby looked up. 'Just like Cyril Jenkins, sir.'

'Just like Cyril Jenkins,' agreed Sloan.

* * *

Later still.

'I've been a fool, Crosby.'

Crosby, no diplomat but still a career man, said guardedly, 'How come, sir?'

'We agreed a long time ago,' (it was Wednesday actually) 'that where Grace Jenkins had gone in her Sunday best on Tuesday was relevant.'

'Yes, sir. Bound to have been. Someone who knew she would arrive at Berebury bus station too late to catch the five-fifteen.'

'So she was bound to catch the seven-five,' Sloan pointed to Crosby's notebook. 'She helped an old lady who fell getting off the bus, didn't she?'

'Yes, sir, but I don't see what . . .'

'The bus company will have the old lady's name and address. You can bet your sweet life on that. It'll be a rule of the house in case of an injury claim afterwards. Ten to one she came off the same bus.'

'Do you think so, sir?'

'It's worth a try.'

*   *   *

It was still Sunday.

That, to Henrietta, was the funniest part. It didn't seem like Sunday at all.

She was trying to explain to Inspector Sloan how it was she knew someone had been into the house during the night, but it didn't seem as if he wanted to know.

'That's all right, miss. I rather thought they might.'

'Inspector, were they looking for me?'

'I think so, miss.'

'You mean I'm in someone's way?'

'Let's say you're the stumbling-block, miss.'

'What to?' Bewildered.

'A pretty penny, miss, though I'd say most of it's gone now.' He raised a hand to stem any more questions. 'Now that we know someone was here, would you mind just not mentioning it to anyone at all please.'

'Bill knows already. He was here . . .'

'To anyone else besides—er—Bill.'

'All right.' She didn't really care very much now whom she spoke to, still less what she said. 'The blood, Inspector, did it tell?'

'Yes, miss.' He paused. 'You're not Cyril Jenkins's daughter after all.'

'No.'

'You're not surprised?'

'No.' She hesitated. 'I think I would have felt it more.'

'Very probably, miss.'

'Affinity. That's the word, isn't it? I didn't feel that when I saw him. He was just a photograph, you see. Not like her.'

Sloan heard the warmth come flooding back into her voice and said as impersonally as he could, 'She really cared for you, miss. I expect that's what makes the difference, more than blood relationships.'

229

'Yes.' She turned her head away. 'Inspector, what about tonight? Do I go back to the Rectory?'

'Ah,' said Sloan. 'Tonight. Now listen very carefully. This is important.'

*   *   *

'No,' said Superintendent Leeyes flatly.

'But, sir . . .'

'Too risky. Suppose the girl gets hurt.'

'She won't be there to be hurt.'

'I still don't like it.'

'I can't think of a better way of making him show his hand.'

There was a long pause. It became evident that the Superintendent couldn't either.

*   *   *

Henrietta was standing in the telephone kiosk outside the post office. It was nearly ten o'clock in the evening.

The fact that the pile of small change feeding the coin box came from Inspector Sloan's pocket was highly significant.

'Is that you, Mr Hibbs? This is Henrietta Jenkins speaking.'

Sloan could hear his deep voice crackling over the line.

'It is.'

'I'm sorry to trouble you but I'd like some

230

advice.'

'What's the trouble?' James Augustus Heber Hibbs, secular adviser to the village, did not sound particularly surprised. Just attentive.

'I was just going to bed,' said Henrietta, 'and I thought I'd like something to read. I . . . I haven't been sleeping all that well since . . .'

'Quite.'

'Well, I was getting a book out of the bookcase—one of my favourites actually—and I came across my mother's will. It's in an envelope—all sealed up. I just wondered what I should do.'

'Put it somewhere safe,' advised Hibbs sensibly, 'and ring your solicitor first thing in the morning.'

She had exactly the same conversation a few minutes later with Felix Arbican.

'Grace Jenkins's will?' echoed the solicitor. 'Are you sure?'

'Quite sure,' said Henrietta mendaciously. 'You said it would be a help.'

'It will,' said Arbican. 'I think you'd better bring it over to me first thing in the morning— just as you found it. In the meantime . . .'

'Yes?' said Henrietta meekly.

'Put it in the bureau.'

'But the lock's gone.'

'I don't suppose anyone would think to go back there a second time.'

Bill Thorpe might have been in bed when Henrietta rang the farm. He didn't say. He

231

listened to her tale and said firmly, 'Before you leave the call box I should ring the police. Let them decide what to do. And then I should go straight back to the Rectory.'

'I'm not going back there tonight,' she said. 'I'll be all right on my own.'

'Now listen to me, Henrietta Jenkins . . .'

'Not Jenkins,' said Henrietta sedately.

'Henrietta whoever you are, I won't have you . . .'

But Henrietta had rung off.

'I meant that,' she said to Sloan.

'What, miss?'

'That bit about not going back to the Rectory.'

'Oh, yes, you are.'

Henrietta smiled sweetly. 'Oh, no, I'm not, Inspector. What's more, you can't make me. I'm coming back to the cottage with you.'

*　　*　　*

For a long time nothing happened.

Henrietta switched lights on and off according to Sloan's bidding—kitchen first, then hall, ten minutes later the bathroom, and finally the bedroom one. Then, fully dressed, she crept downstairs again.

'Please, miss,' pleaded Sloan, 'won't you go and lie down in the spare room? If anything happens to you I shall be in for the high jump.'

'What's going to happen?' she asked.

'I don't know,' he said truthfully, 'but we're dealing with a confirmed murderer.'

'Inspector . . .' Henrietta found it easier to talk in the dark. She had the feeling that she was alone with Sloan though she knew Constable Crosby was in the next room and PC Hepple in the kitchen and heaven knew who outside. 'Inspector, do you know now who I am?'

'Yes, miss, I think so. We'll have to check with Somerset House in the morning, but . . .'

'Who?' she asked directly.

'Henrietta Mantriot.'

'Mantriot.' She tested out the sound, tentative as a bride with a new surname. 'Henrietta Eleanor Leslie Mantriot.'

'Your mother . . .' began Sloan.

'Yes?' There was a sudden constriction in her voice.

'We think she was called Eleanor Leslie. The spelling of Leslie ought to have given us a clue.'

'I've often wondered,' she remarked, 'where those names came from.'

'She's been dead a long time,' volunteered Sloan.

This did not seem to disturb the girl. 'I knew she must have been,' she said, 'otherwise Grace Jenkins wouldn't have . . .'

'No.'

'And my father, Inspector?'

'Your father, miss, we think was a certain

233

Captain Hugo Mantriot.'

'Master Hugo!' she cried.

'Shhhhhhsh, miss. We must be very quiet now.'

'I'm sorry,' she said contritely. 'I was always hearing about Master Hugo. I never dreamt that . . .'

'Now you know why, miss.' Sloan heard Crosby's whisper before Henrietta did and he was on his feet and out in the hall in a flash.

'Someone coming down the Belling road, sir.'

'Upstairs,' commanded Sloan. 'Quickly. You too, miss.'

In the end he went up with her and stood at the landing window. Together they watched someone approach the cottage on foot, slide open the gate and disappear behind some bushes in the garden.

'He's not coming in,' whispered Henrietta.

'Not yet,' murmured Sloan. 'Give him time. He's waiting to see if the coast's clear.' He withdrew from the window and passed the word down to Crosby and Hepple to be very quiet now.

It was quite still inside Boundary Cottage.

The next move was a complete surprise to everyone.

Constable Crosby's hoarse whisper reached Sloan and Henrietta on the front upstairs landing.

'There's someone else, sir.'

'Where?'

'Coming down the Belling Road.'

The visitor did not pause in the garden. He came straight up to the front door.

'Inspector,' said Henrietta. 'Look! The man in the garden. He's following the other one in.'

Sloan did not stay to reply. He moved back to the head of the stairs and waited there, watching the front door open.

'He's got a key,' breathed Henrietta, hearing it being inserted into the lock.

"Shhhhhsh,' cautioned Sloan. 'Don't speak now.'

The front door opened soundlessly and someone came in. Whoever it was moved forward and then turned to shut the door behind him.

Only it wouldn't shut.

And it wouldn't shut for a time-honoured reason. There was someone else's foot in it.

Someone pushed from the inside and someone else pushed from the outside. The outside pusher must have been the stronger of the two for in the end the door opened wide enough to admit him.

Henrietta recognised the silhouette dimly outlined against the night sky and framed by the doorway. She clutched the banister rail for support. No wonder he had got the door opened in spite of the other man. Bill Thorpe was the strongest man she knew.

Bill Thorpe was apparently not content with

having got the door open. He now advanced upon the other man, flinging himself against him. There was a surprised grunt, followed by a muffled oath. Then a different sound, the sudden ripping of cloth. In the darkness it sounded like a pistol shot.

It was enough for Detective Inspector Sloan.

He switched on the lights.

'The police!' cried a somewhat dishevelled Felix Arbican. 'Thank God for that. I caught this young man breaking into . . .'

'Felix Forrest Arbican,' said Sloan awfully from half-way up the stairs. 'I arrest you for the murder of Cyril Edgar Jenkins and must warn you that anything you say may be . . .'

'Thank you,' retorted the solicitor coldly, 'I am aware of the formula.'

CHAPTER NINETEEN

'I thought it would be the solicitor,' said Superintendent Leeyes unfairly. 'Bound to be when you came to think about it.'

'Yes, sir.' Sloan was sitting in the Superintendent's office the next morning, turning in his report.

'What put you onto him in the beginning, Sloan?'

'It was the very first time we saw him, sir. I

asked him if he knew of a client called Mrs G. E. Jenkins and he said no.'

'And?'

'And in the interview he referred to her as Grace Jenkins though neither Crosby nor I had mentioned her Christian name, so I reckoned he knew her all right.'

Leeyes grunted. 'Stroke of bad luck that Hibbs fellow keeping his letter all those years.'

'Yes and no, sir. He'd written it a bit ambiguously at the time—it could indicate a settlement like he said if you cared to look at it that way, so it could have been said to have served his case as well.' He paused. 'I think he would know that an agent would file it, too. Besides . . .'

'Besides what?'

'It was a sort of insurance, sir. If we should get hold of it, it would bring him into the picture and keep him in touch in a rather privileged way, wouldn't it?'

Leeyes grunted again.

'That's why I told the girl about him early on,' said Sloan.

'You did what?'

'Sort of hinted that he was her mother's solicitor and so . . .' Sloan waved a hand and left the sentence unfinished.

'Suppose,' suggested Leeyes heavily, 'we go back to the very beginning.'

'The last war,' said Sloan promptly. 'A promising young officer in the East Calleshires called Hugo Mantriot of Great Rooden Manor . . .'

'Where's that?'

'Just south of Calleford.' Sloan resumed his narrative. 'This Hugo Mantriot marries the only daughter of the late Bruce Leslie . . .'

'Who's he?'

'The shipping magnate.'

'Money?'

'Lots.'

Leeyes nodded, satisfied.

'They have a baby girl,' went on Sloan.

'Henrietta?'

'Henrietta Eleanor Leslie Mantriot.' Sloan paused. 'When she's about six weeks old her father comes home on leave to Great Rooden and there's a terrible—er—accident.'

'What?' bluntly.

'According to the reports at the time Captain Hugo Mantriot went completely out of his mind, shot his wife and then himself. The Coroner was very kind—said some soothing sentences about the man's mind being turned by his wartime experiences and so forth. The whole thing played down as much as possible, of course.'

Leeyes grunted.

'Twenty-four people had been killed by a flying bomb in Calleford the same week—the police had more than enough to do—the Coroner hinted that the Mantriots were really casualties of war in very much the same way as the flying bomb victims . . .'

'Arbican kill them both?' suggested Leeyes briefly.

'I shouldn't wonder, sir, at all, though we're not likely to find out at this stage.' Sloan turned over a new page in his notebook. 'Mrs Mantriot had made a new will when the baby was born. I've had someone turn it up for me in Somerset House this morning and read it out. She created a trust for the baby should anything happen to either parent . . .'

'She being at risk as much as he was in those days,' put in Leeyes, who could remember them.

'Exactly, sir. Those were the days when things did happen to people, besides which her husband was on active service and there was a fair bit of money involved. So she created this trust with the trustees as . . .'

'Don't tell me,' groaned Leeyes.

'That's right, sir. Waind, Arbican and Waind. After that, of course, it's only guesswork on my part . . .'

'Well?'

'I reckon Grace Jenkins was already in the employment of the Mantriots as the baby's nanny. She was a daughter of Jenkins at Holly Tree Farm in Rooden Parva which isn't all that far away . . .'

'So?'

'I think Arbican suggested to her that she look after the baby. Probably put it into her mind that the infant shouldn't be told about the murder and suicide of her parents—that would seem a pretty disgraceful thing to a simple country girl like her.'

Leeyes grunted.

'From there,' said Sloan, 'it's a fairly easy step to getting her to pass the baby off as her own until the child was twenty-one. All done with the highest motives, of course.'

'Of course,' agreed Leeyes. 'And he keeps them both, I suppose?'

'That's right. Sets Grace Jenkins up in a remote cottage, maintains the household at a distance and not very generously at that . . .'

'Verisimilitude,' said Leeyes.

'Pardon, sir?'

'You wouldn't expect a widow and child to have a lot of money.'

'No, sir, of course not. Grace Jenkins falls for it like a lamb. Takes along a photograph of her own brother to forestall questions, and Hugo Mantriot's medals, and puts her back into bringing up Master Hugo's baby as if it's her own.'

'Then what?'

'Then nothing, sir, for nearly twenty-one years. During which time the Wainds in the firm die off, public memory dies down and Felix Arbican gets through a fair slice of what Bruce Leslie left his daughter.'

'The day of reckoning,' said Leeyes slowly, 'would be Henrietta's twenty-first birthday.'

'That's right. Grace Jenkins had no intention of carrying the pretence further than that. She was a loyal servant and an honest woman.'

'So?'

'She had to go,' said Sloan simply, 'and before Henrietta came back from university.'

*   *   *

'He just overlooked the one thing,' said Sloan.

It was the afternoon now and Sloan and Crosby were sitting in the Rectory drawing-room. In spite of all her protestations Henrietta had gone to the Rectory the previous night—or rather, in the early hours of the morning—after all. Bill Thorpe and PC Hepple had escorted her there to make—as Sloan said at the time—assurance doubly sure. Once there Mrs Meyton had taken it upon herself to protect her from all comers and she had been allowed to sleep on through the morning.

Now they were all foregathered in the Rectory again—bar the main contestant, so to speak. The case was nearly over, the Rectory china looked suitably unfragile and Mrs Meyton's tea-pot as if it contained tea of a properly dark brown hue—so Sloan had consented to a cup.

'Just the one thing,' he repeated.

Nobody took a lot of notice. Henrietta and

Bill Thorpe were looking at each other as if for the very first time. Mrs Meyton was counting cups. Constable Crosby seemed preoccupied with a large bruise that was coming up on his right knuckle.

'What was that?' asked Mr Meyton with Christian kindness.

'That a routine post-mortem would establish the fact of Grace Jenkins's childlessness.'

'Otherwise?'

'Otherwise I doubt if we would have looked further than a Road Traffic Accident. We wouldn't have had any reason to.'

'Then what?' put in Bill Thorpe.

'Then nothing very much,' said Sloan. 'Inspector Harpe would have added it to his list of unsolved hit-and-runs and that would have been that. Miss Mantriot would . . .'

Henrietta looked quite startled. 'No one's ever called me that before.'

Sloan smiled and continued. 'Miss Mantriot would have gone back to university none the wiser. She's twenty-one next month. The only likely occasion for her to need a birth certificate after that would be for a passport.'

Bill Thorpe nodded. 'And if it wasn't forthcoming, she wouldn't even know where to begin to look.'

'Exactly.'

'Hamstrung,' said Bill Thorpe expressively.

'But,' said Henrietta, 'what about her telling

me she had been a Miss Wright before she married?'

Sloan's expression relaxed a little. 'I never met Grace Jenkins, miss, but I've—well—come to respect her quite a bit in the last week. I think she had what you might call an ironic sense of humour. This Wright business . . .'

'Yes?'

'I expect you've all heard the expression about Mr Right coming along.'

Henrietta coloured. 'Yes.'

'Me,' said Bill Thorpe brightly.

'Perhaps,' said Sloan. 'In her case I think when she had to choose a maiden name so to speak—she chose Wright in reverse.'

'Well done, Grace Jenkins,' said Mr Meyton.

'That's what I think too, sir,' said Sloan. 'The same thing applies in a way with the Hocklington-Garwells who had us running round in circles for a bit.'

'What about it?'

'When she had to choose the name of a family she'd worked for—you know the sort of questions children ask, and she couldn't very well say Mantriot—I think she put together the names of two people involved in an old Calleshire scandal.'

'Hocklington and Garwell?'

'That's right. I gather it was a pretty well-known affair in the county in the old days.'

243

'That's how Mrs Hibbs knew about it!' said Crosby suddenly.

'I didn't know you'd noticed,' said his superior kindly, 'but you're quite right.'

'But it had nothing to do with the case at all?' said the Rector, anxious to get at least one thing quite clear.

'Nothing,' said Sloan.

'So there was a reason why she was older than I thought,' said Henrietta.

Sloan nodded. 'And for her having her hair dyed and for her not liking having her photograph taken.'

'And for Cyril Jenkins having to be killed,' said Bill Thorpe logically.

'He was her brother. And, of course, he knew the whole story. As far as Grace Jenkins was concerned there was no reason why he shouldn't.'

'So he had to die,' concluded Mr Meyton.

'Once I'd seen him,' cried Henrietta. 'He was quite safe until then.'

'Not really, miss. You see, he would have known about your going to be told the truth when you were twenty-one. He'd have smelt a rat about his sister's death before very long.' He paused. 'That's what put James Hibbs in the clear for once and for all.'

'What did?'

'He didn't know you'd seen Cyril Jenkins so there was no call for him to be killing him on Saturday afternoon.'

'I hadn't thought of that . . .'

'The only people who knew were young Mr Thorpe here, Arbican himself . . .'

'I told him,' said Henrietta, with a shudder.

'And Mr and Mrs Meyton here.'

'How did you know it wasn't me?' enquired Bill Thorpe with deep interest.

'I couldn't be quite sure. Especially when you turned up last night.'

'I wasn't going to come in,' said Thorpe somewhat bashfully. 'I just wanted to keep an eye on the place. Besides, I didn't have a key.'

'*He* had,' said Henrietta. She meant Arbican but didn't seem able to say the name.

'Yes, miss, he had. Had it for years, I expect. He used that when he came in on Tuesday. He had to make sure Grace Jenkins hadn't left anything incriminating around. He probably took your birth certificate away with him then and anything else that might have given the game away.'

'Inspector,' Henrietta pushed back a wayward strand of hair. 'What did happen on Tuesday?'

'We can't be quite sure but I should imagine Arbican summoned Grace Jenkins over to Calleford for a conference. You can imagine the sort of thing. "Henrietta's coming home— she's twenty-one next month—got to be told— modest celebration" and so forth.'

Henrietta winced.

'That would explain the Sunday best that so

puzzled Mrs Callows and Mrs Ricks,' said Sloan, 'and her catching the early bus into Berebury and the last bus back. Berebury to Calleford is a very slow run, you know. The bus calls at all the villages on the way.'

'He wouldn't have her to his office, surely?'

'No. I expect he took her out to lunch, then put her on the bus back which he knew would get her into Berebury after the five-fifteen to Larking had left.'

'So he knew she would be on the seven-five?'

'That's right. Then he drives himself cross country. It's a much shorter run. First he goes through the bureau and then waits in the pub car park until the bus gets in. He would be able to see her get off. All he has to do then is to time her walk until she's near enough to the bad corner for it to seem like a nasty accident.'

'Which it wasn't,' said Henrietta.

'No, miss.'

'Inspector,' the Rector spoke up. 'What was Arbican's motive in all this?'

'Gain,' said Sloan succinctly. 'Carefully calculated and very expertly carried out. Unless he confesses we shall never know whether he contrived the deaths of Henrietta's father and mother. It isn't impossible and they happened very smartly after the legal arrangements had been completed, but there is another death we do know something about now . . .'

246

'Cyril Jenkins, you mean?'

'Him, too, sir,' Sloan said to the Rector, 'but that was afterwards. This one was before Grace Jenkins was killed.'

It was very quiet in the Rectory drawing-room.

'Who was that, Inspector?'

'A certain Miss Winifred Lendry, sir.'

'I've never heard of her,' said Mr Meyton.

'I don't suppose any of you have.' Sloan looked round the room. 'It is her death that makes us realise that this was all a long-term plan. Miss Lendry was Arbican's confidential secretary until she was killed by a hit-and-run driver last autumn.'

*   *   *

It was on the Thursday morning that Constable Crosby picked up the telephone and handed the receiver to Detective Inspector Sloan.

'For you, sir. The Kinnisport police.'

'Good morning,' said Sloan.

'About this Major Hocklington,' began his opposite number in Kinnisport. 'Do you want us to watch him for ever? I've had a man posted outside his house for days now and the old boy hasn't stepped out of his wheel-chair once . . .'

We hope you have enjoyed this Large Print book. Other Chivers Press or G.K. Hall & Co. Large Print books are available at your library or directly from the publishers.

For more information about current and forthcoming titles, please call or write, without obligation, to:

Chivers Press Limited
Windsor Bridge Road
Bath BA2 3AX
England
Tel. (01225) 335336

OR

G.K. Hall & Co.
P.O. Box 159
Thorndike, Maine 04986
USA
Tel. (800) 223-2336

All our Large Print titles are designed for easy reading, and all our books are made to last.